Gypsy
at
Heart

ELLEN DUGAN

This is a work of fiction. Names, characters, organizations, places, events, and incidents are either products of the author's imagination or are used fictitiously.

Copyright © 2016 Ellen Dugan

Published by Ellen Dugan

Edited by Katherine Pace

Cover art by Dar Albert

ISBN: 978-1541015463

TITLES BY ELLEN DUGAN

NON-FICTION TITLES

Garden Witchery: Magick from the Ground Up (2004 COVR Award Winner)

Elements of Witchcraft: Natural Magick for Teens

Cottage Witchery: Natural Magick for Hearth & Home

Autumn Equinox: The Enchantment of Mabon

The Enchanted Cat: Feline Fascinations, Spells & Magick (2007 COVR Winner)

Herb Magic for Beginners: Down to-Earth Enchantments

Natural Witchery Intuitive, Personal & Practical Magick (2008 COVR Award Winner)

How to Enchant a Man: Spells to Bewitch, Bedazzle & Beguile

Garden Witch's Herbal: Green Magick, Herbalism & Spirituality (2010 COVR Award Winner)

Book of Witchery: Spells, Charms & Correspondences For Every Day of the Week

Practical Protection Magick: Guarding & Reclaiming Your Power

Seasons of Witchery: Celebrating the Sabbats with the Garden Witch

Witches Tarot- Deck and Book Kit

Garden Witchery 10th Anniversary Edition

Practical Prosperity Magick: Crafting Success & Abundance

Every Witch Way-- written with Tess Whitehurst

The Natural Psychic: Ellen Dugan's Personal Guide to the Psychic Realm

FICTION TITLES

LEGACY OF MAGICK SERIES
Legacy of Magick
Secret of the Rose
Message Of The Crow
Beneath An Ivy Moon
Under the Holly Moon

THE GYPSY CHRONICLES
Gypsy At Heart

Ki shan i Romani—
Adoi san' i chov'hani.
"Wherever gypsies go,
There the witches are, we know."
~Old Familiar Saying

CONTENTS

ACKNOWLEDGMENTS

A word of appreciation to Barbara for her generosity, friendship and for the formatting.

To my daughter, Erin, who found herself working in the office of a funeral home after grad school. Thanks for the behind the scenes look. And even though you were very surprised at running into the spirits of the recently departed— I wasn't. It only made me smile to realize that we had another Psychic-Medium in the family. Love you Sis!

CHAPTER ONE

You would've thought, considering my heritage, that I would have seen this coming...but the last place I would have ever predicted to be working, was at a funeral home.

With my Masters Degree in education hot off the presses, I had expected to be working in my chosen field. But after six months of trying to find a full-time teaching job, I was *still* in retail hell at the local mall. As my student loans were looming large, I had begun applying for anything that would get me out of the clothing store chain which led to me sending in a resume to an old, established family business in my hometown of Danvers.

That's how I ended up at the Fogg Funeral Home. I needed a good full-time job with benefits—and they were hiring. I reminded myself of those few facts as I parked my car. I was damn lucky to have gotten this job in the current economy. The pay was amazing, the hours good, and most of the people I worked with were pretty easy going and quiet. As in *dead quiet*. I chuckled at my inner monologue and turned off the car.

Funeral home humor. It never gets old.

I opened my car door, stood, and sighed in resignation. The late October sun filtered down through the branches of a golden-leafed maple tree, and I lifted my face to the light. It was probably going to be the only time today I'd have the chance to enjoy feeling the sun on my skin.

I shrugged on my black blazer, hitched my new purse over my arm, and remembered my lunch at the last second. I shut the car door with my hip, squared my shoulders for yet another thrilling day and started the walk across the parking lot in my practical flats.

I waved at the gardener. The older man was working in the manicured flower beds of the funeral home. I'd seen him nearly every morning since the first day I'd started two months ago. We usually exchanged a quick word and *Old Joe*, as he'd told me to call him, kept me on my toes by using random phrases and greetings in Polish.

Thanks to my grandmother, I could

understand most of what he said. Plus, I could admit that it was becoming a sort of personal challenge: Me trying to translate on the fly and him trying to set me up with his grandson. Talking to Old Joe had become the highlight of my day.

"*Dzień dobry*, Nilah," he said, straightening from where he'd been meticulously trimming the boxwood hedges.

"Good morning, Joe." I stopped and smiled at the older man. "The chrysanthemums are looking good," I said, gesturing to the mounds of yellow flowers at his feet.

"They are," he agreed. "So, how's your love life?"

"Grandma Sabina says that I'll meet a tall dark stranger any day now." I tucked my tongue in my cheek. "But I've told her, my heart belongs to you."

That made him throw back his head and roar with laughter, for a couple of reasons. First, my grandmother is a professional fortune teller—an honest to god Gypsy fortune teller. *Polska Roma* to be exact. And secondly, the branches of my family tree were thick with psychics, astrologers, and folk magicians. *Except for one branch, anyway.*

"How is your *babcia*?" he asked.

"My grandmother is fine." I said. The breeze had strands of my brown, wavy hair escaping the low bun I'd tried to tame it in to. "This is her busy season. First from the leaf peepers in September, and especially now with Halloween almost here."

"I'll bet." Old Joe tugged his ball cap more firmly on his head. His salt and pepper hair tufted out around his ears.

"Yeah," I agreed with a sigh. "Lots of tourists have been hitting Danvers, hoping to have their cards, palms, and tea leaves read. She's been busy for the past few weeks." *And hopefully too busy to have kept up with her latest project.* I thought to myself. *Which was namely trying to play matchmaker to her last unmarried granddaughter: me.*

"You need to meet my grandson, Joseph," Old Joe said, as he usually did. "He was named after me. You'd be perfect for each other."

I dodged the latest matchmaking attempt with a good humored shrug. "Are you trying to break my heart?" I asked him, tucking the loose strands of my hair behind my ear. "I thought you and I were going on a date this weekend?"

Old Joe shook his head at me. "You better go on inside now. *Miłego dnia.*"

I knew that one! "You 'have a nice day', too." I waved and hustled into the side entrance of the funeral home.

The huge, three-story mansion was brick and built in 1879. At some point in the past it had been painted white, which I personally thought was a damn shame. The old gothic house now turned funeral home was constructed in the Second Empire style of architecture. The sculpted details around the windows and dormers added formality and charm. The building had a mansard roof in soft gray, and was topped with ornate iron trim.

I let myself in through the employee entrance, tucked my lunch in the break room fridge, and took the back stairs up to my third floor office. Like the rest of the building, my office was tastefully decorated as I supposed someone considered appropriate for a funeral home. Personally, I thought it was as mind-numbingly dull and almost as boring as the uniforms all the employee's had to wear.

While the job itself was fine, the dress code was stifling. To be honest, I think my family was more shocked with my work attire than with *where* I worked. The funeral home uniform of a white blouse, black skirt and blazer for the female employees was staid, dreary and unimaginative. Honestly, the uniform had been starting to make me feel like a frumpy old librarian.

My curves—I prefer to think of them as generous—were hidden behind a black blazer and knee length skirt. It's tough to find nicely cut clothes when you wear what is classified as a, 'plus size', and the outfit was not flattering on me. Not in cut or color. If anything, it made me look rounder instead of shapely.

The company policy of wearing subtle cosmetics, didn't compliment my medium complexion either. My brown hair and hazel eyes needed bolder colors and jewel tones to stand out. Still, I was determined to not let the uniform get me down. Checking my hair in the large mirror inside my office door, I secured a few bobby pins in the bun at the nape of my neck, and then tightened the back on a drop style Baltic amber earring. The slight dangle of the earring, was walking the line, and would put me at risk of violating the 'discreet jewelry' dress code.

"You're living on the edge, Nilah," I said to my reflection.

Recently I had begun a little rebellion against the company dress code. This week in addition to the earrings, I was trying new cosmetics. I pulled a tube of lip gloss out of my purse and slid some deep mauve over my lips. I studied my reflection and decided the new eye shadow had been a good investment. The deeper tones of mauve-brown *did* make my hazel eyes appear a tad greener.

Today, besides the new eye shadow and the drop earrings, I was carrying a big, pumpkin-orange pleather purse. The handbag featured silver studs and fringe. It was sassy and bright, and when I sat it on my desk it seemed like a colorful declaration of the season (or maybe war). It was, quite frankly, the only colorful and stylish thing in the office. *Can't tame this Gypsy's heart,* I thought a bit dramatically as I tucked away the lip gloss.

I booted up my computer, and noticed several forms waiting for me in the inbox on my desk, which meant another thrilling day of filling out and then filing death certificates for the state of Massachusetts. That, and doing whatever else the funeral director needed done. Or god help me— whatever his bleached blonde wife thought I should be doing.

I'd no sooner sat behind my desk, when the funeral director's wife, Alicia Fogg, strolled past my doorway with a large pink and white floral arrangement of gladiolas and calla lilies.

"Morning Alicia," I said, figuring she was probably recycling some left behind floral arrangements. She spotted me, backed up, and set the arrangement on a console table in the hall.

Alicia Fogg wore her slim black skirt and tailored jacket to perfection. Of course they looked great on her, she was a size two on a bad day, *and* she could afford designer clothes. Her snowy blouse was silk and a single strand of pearls hung around her neck. She was ice-cold, movie star beautiful, and bitchy.

As if to confirm the *bitchy* part of my analysis, she stared down her nose at me. "Good morning, Nilah," she said, mispronouncing my name for the umpteenth time.

"Nile-ah," I enunciated slowly. "My name is pronounced Nile-ah. Not *Nill-uh* like the cookie." I said, determined to be cheerful. "If it helps, think of the river Nile with an *ah* sound on the end."

Alicia lowered her over plucked eyebrows and huffed out a breath. "Right," she said dismissively and I watched her pale blue eyes zero in on my purse. "That's certainly a bright color."

I patted the handbag. "Yes, I do love bright colors and it's so festive with Halloween coming up."

"Your purse should be on the floor, not sitting on the desk," Alicia said.

"If you put your purse on the floor—you'll have no money," I said automatically, and then regretted it as she puckered up again.

"Is that a Gypsy thing?" Alicia asked suspiciously.

I smiled, but didn't mean it. "It's an old Polish..." I stopped and reconsidered my words. "Tradition," I finally said.

Watch it, Nilah! I reminded myself. *The woman*

would probably blow a gasket if you'd have said, 'folk magick'. Trying to act casual, I plucked up my purse and tucked it in the middle drawer of my desk. I smoothed the fringe down and slid the drawer shut.

Alicia's shoulders dropped, as if the mere absence of my bright, fringed purse was helping her to relax. "That's better. Much less distracting."

I resisted the urge to roll my eyes. I tucked a strand of hair back behind my ear. "Well, then, I'll get to work."

"Are you wearing drop style earrings?" Alicia tilted her head to one side. "What stone is that?" she asked.

Apparently, my little rebellion against the company dress code had not *gone unnoticed after all.* "It's amber. Baltic amber," I answered.

"I didn't know amber could be almost red in color."

"Baltic amber comes in a lot of colors," I said.

Alicia pursed her lips. "It's more valuable in that color, isn't it?"

And here we go...mystery solved as to why she was still speaking to me. "Yes," I said. "The earrings were a gift from my grandmother."

"Well, you may wear them to work. But please, check the dress code again and refrain from anymore displays of garish colors in your accessories."

I blinked at her words, and bit my lip to keep from laughing. She was still lecturing me on the dress code, but her next words had me snapping to attention.

"...and I suppose you simply can't help yourself, what with your people and all," Alicia said with a sigh.

I braced my arms against the desk, and turned to regard her. "Can't help myself with what?" I asked very carefully.

Alicia's hand fluttered to her throat. "I meant, you know... your predilection for flashy colors," she said. "That's a cultural thing, right?"

Growing up, I'd taken a lot of jabs at my Gypsy heritage. As an adult, very few pissed me off, but this one came close. I ignored her comment, and smiled slowly at her, deciding to give as good as I got. "Wow, your hair looks great today, Alicia." I said sweetly. "The hairdresser sure did a good job touching up your roots."

She sucked in a breath at the faintly disguised insult. She picked up the arrangement again, and clipped off down the hall in her Louis Vuitton shoes without another word.

I grinned at her retreating back. My phone rang on my desk, and I picked it up. "Hello."

"Nilah." Tommy Hamilton, our resident

embalmer's voice boomed through the receiver. Tommy was one of the few people who worked at the funeral home that I actually enjoyed. He was warm and outgoing, with a fabulous sense of humor, and he took great pride and care in his work. He was dating one of the receptionists named Joanna. "Hey, I've got some exciting news!" he said.

"Don't tell me, let me guess... A zombie apocalypse has broken out?" I asked cheerfully.

"Ha!" Tommy laughed. "No, even better! I asked Jo to marry me and she said yes!"

"That's wonderful!" I said. "I'm really happy for you."

"Your grandmother Sabina, she told me I should propose this weekend... something about the full moon?"

"That certainly sounds like my grandmother."

"So..." Tommy trailed off. "You got any predictions on *when* we should get married?"

And just like that—my good mood disappeared. "Tommy," I began. "I wouldn't know. I don't have the gifts that my grandmother does."

"Oh." I could hear the confusion in his voice. "I'm sorry. I assumed since your grandmother, mother, and your sister were all are psychics— that you were too."

"Nope." I tried to sound pleasant, but I was

pretty sure I sounded grim instead. "Anyway, congratulations on your engagement."

"Thanks, Nilah," Tommy said. "Talk to you later." He disconnected and I took a deep breath, working for calm. I picked up the form to issue a death certificate and stared at it blindly.

My grandmother, Sabina Abrams had indeed been working as a professional fortune teller since she was a young woman. After her husband passed away she had supported her family with her talents, and she'd built a solid reputation for being an honest and *accurate* psychic. She passed on that trade to my mother, Nadia, and they in turn tried to teach me and my younger sister Vanessa. Vanessa had taken to it naturally, but I, however, was a spectacular failure.

I had zero occult talents as far as anyone could see. Even the simplest of folk magick practices flopped—if I tried them. Astrology confused the hell out of me, and I had no skills at palmistry. I loved the art and images of the tarot... but bombed when I tried to do readings for the public. My tea leaf reading, tasseography, was so-so. Again I had the symbolism down cold but, the art of divination was so much more than simply memorizing the symbols and the meanings.

There needed to be a psychic *connection,* a spark of magick, or at the very least some psychic intuition between the client and the reader. I'd worked hard, and then waited all my life for my psychic abilities to present themselves. But I'd waited in vain. So I'd turned my attention and energy to academia.

I knew that my family loved me, but yet I'd always been treated as if I was suffering from some type of slight developmental disability. The whole, "we love you, no matter what," thing.

Now here I was, working a mundane job at the local funeral home, trying to chip away at a ton of student debt. My parents were relieved that I'd finally landed a decent job with benefits, my brothers thought my job was hilarious, and my grandmother... I don't think she approved of where I worked at all. She seemed to be watching me very closely these days.

But then again, I was still single. It was a toss up as to what upset her more. My current job, or that I was an *unmarried* female at the ripe old age of twenty six, with no discernable psychic abilities or magickal talents of any kind.

My name is Nilah Stefanik, and I am the disgrace of my Gypsy family.

CHAPTER TWO

I spent the morning slogging my way through paperwork and official files for the state. When I came up for air, I went downstairs to fill in for Joanna, the receptionist, so she could have her lunch break with Tommy. I complimented her on the new engagement ring on her finger, and took position behind the front desk. There were two visitations scheduled for the afternoon and even though the families hadn't arrived yet, I was kept busy directing floral deliveries, manning the phone, and answering questions about the services.

"Yes, the visitation begins at 3:00 pm," I said to the caller. I glanced up to find an elderly woman standing in front of the desk. I jolted a little as I hadn't seen, or even heard her come in through the main doors. "Well, hello," I said, hanging up the phone.

Her hair was snowy white, and curly. She smiled at me, flashing her dentures. "You're Nilah Stephanik?" she asked.

I smiled back automatically. With the big name tag I was wearing on my lapel, it didn't surprise me that she knew my name. But it was rare for people to pronounce my name correctly. "Yes, Ma'am," I answered. "I'm Nilah. May I help you?"

"I'm searching for my family. Can you tell me where they are?"

The visitations didn't begin for a few hours and I guessed she was early. "Who are you here to see?" I asked, checking the paperwork in front of me. We had two visitations today; one for a Mr. Mortimer Adams and the second for a Mrs. Elizabeth Samuel.

"I'm here to see *you*, young lady." She huffed out an impatient breath. "Can you help me contact my family or not?"

Despite myself, I smiled at her impatient tone. The woman was small, thin and appeared to be well into her late eighties if not early nineties. Her faded blue eyes seemed clear however, and matched the pale blue jacket dress she wore. A double strand of pearls hung around her neck, and a large silver pin decorated her dress. The brooch was done in a floral motif, was studded with pearls, and centered with a pale blue stone. For some reason she put me in mind of the Queen of England.

I wondered if she was a little confused. *Poor thing,* I thought and sincerely hoped she wasn't alone. "What's your name Ma'am?"

"I'm Lizzie," she said with a decisive nod.

"Okay Lizzie, let's see if we can't figure out where your family is." I tried to sound reassuring. Then the phone on the desk began to ring. "Give me a second, while I answer this." I snatched up the phone. "Fogg Funeral Home, please hold." I punched the hold button and turned back to Lizzie.

She was gone.

I scanned the main lobby and saw no one. I dropped the phone back in the cradle and took off and down the main hall of the first floor. The restrooms were on the lower level, and I doubted that she could have gotten down the steps that quickly. To the left and right there were large parlors. The caskets were in place, and the Service Assistants were setting up. I checked the room on the right, the Harbor Room, and I saw flowers being delivered and arranged around the casket.

I dashed back across the hall to the Ocean Room. Here, a white casket was surrounded by arrangements—all in shades of pink. A large coordinating casket spray of candy pink roses, hot pink gerbera daisies, and pastel snapdragons were being set into place by Franklin Fogg the owner, and funeral director. "Franklin," I called out quietly from the doorway. "Is anyone else in here with you?"

The director turned to me. "No, it's only me and Mrs. Samuel."

"Okay," I said walking over to him. "There was an elderly woman up front a little bit ago, and she was asking for her family. I guess she left."

Franklin, like his wife, wore his designer clothes to perfection. He was gym-toned and handsome with salt and pepper hair. His summer tan had yet to fade and it made his blue eyes seem warmer. Where his wife lacked any and all kindness or compassion, Franklin made up for it in spades. I'd discovered that he was a caring man, and one who took real pride in his work.

He moved to the right to adjust the easel holding a large spray of flowers, and as he did, I glanced over at the open casket. A woman with white curly hair, wearing a pale blue jacket and dress rested there. My heart thudded hard in my chest as I noticed the strands of pearls and the large silver floral shaped brooch, studded with a blue stone and more pearls that was pinned to the dress.

I must have made a little sound, as Franklin turned to me and placed a gentle hand on my elbow. "Elizabeth Samuels," he said, gesturing towards the casket. "She was ninety years old and served in World War II as a nurse."

"Oh," I managed. Staring at the woman I'd just spoken to a few moments before.

As if from a great distance I heard Franklin continue speaking. "...had four children, twelve grandchildren and three great-grandchildren."

"You said her name was Elizabeth?" I asked, feeling a bit faint. *Hadn't I thought she'd sort of reminded me of Queen Elizabeth?* I managed to squelch an inappropriate giggle.

"Yes, her name was Elizabeth." Franklin raised his eyebrows at me as I stood there gaping at the deceased. "But her family called her Lizzie."

Lizzie. I gulped, hard. I took a step back from the casket and began to ease my way out of the room. "I need to get back to the front desk," I said, and walked as quickly as was polite out of the parlor, past the other Service Assistants, and blindly back to my post.

I dropped into the chair behind the desk and blinked away the white and black spots before my eyes. My stomach growled loudly, and I pressed my hand to it.

"Must be low blood sugar," I muttered to

myself. "That would make anyone loopy." The front desk phone rang and I automatically answered. A short time later and the Greeters had begun to arrive, and Joanna came to take over.

One of the Greeters, a woman named Dorothy gave my shoulder a pat as I came around the desk. "Sweetie, you're pale. Are you feeling okay?" she asked.

Dorothy was in her seventies, she called everybody *sweetie*. I flashed the older woman a false smile. "I'm fine, probably need to eat something."

She wagged a finger at me. "You shouldn't skip meals, sweetie."

I nodded and, with no small sense of relief, went directly to the lunchroom to eat my PB and J. I kept my mind blank, eating deliberately. By the time that I'd finished, I had almost convinced myself, that I had simply imagined the whole thing.

I nodded politely to the other employees and went back up to my office. Shutting the door behind me, I shrugged out of my jacket. I hung my blazer on a peg by the door, turned around and yelped.

"Well," the old woman said, folding her arms across her pale blue dress.

I backed up against the door. "You're not

real," I managed.

"I'm talking to you, aren't I?"

Desperately, I shut my eyes. "I'm seeing things."

"How in the hell can you see things if your eyes are shut?" she said.

I cracked open one eye. There she stood. It was definitely the same woman I'd seen downstairs, first at the desk and then *in the casket*...Elizabeth Samuels, wearing the pale blue dress and jacket. She stood besides my desk with her white curly hair, pearl necklace, and jeweled pin, tapping her foot, apparently peeved at the world in general.

I opened my mouth. No sound came out, so I tried again. "Mrs. Samuels?"

"Call me Lizzie," she said.

"I...I don't understand," I stammered. "I saw you in your casket. You're *dead*."

"I figured that out for myself, as I'm standing here in the Fogg Funeral Home, wearing my best Sunday dress." Lizzie sighed. "So I'm the first for you, then?"

"The first?" I asked, clutching my stomach. My lunch was so *not* sitting well.

"The first visitation you've experienced?"

Visitation? My mind raced. *Maybe this was an elaborate hoax—a nasty trick played on the new employees.* I stared at her and tried to decide what to do. Mrs. Samuels looked real enough, so I forced myself to ease away from the door, and slowly reached out to touch her shoulder.

My hand passed right through her.

I squeaked and recoiled from the cold. "Oh my god. You're a..."

Lizzie rolled her eyes at me. "Yes dear, I'm a ghost."

"Holy shit!"

"Watch your language, young lady," Lizzie said.

I apologized automatically. I stared hard at her but she was still there, watching me. "This can't be happening," I muttered.

Lizzie glared at me. "You think *you're* surprised?"

I shook my head as my mind began to catch up with the situation. "Lizzie, why are you here? Why are you talking to me?"

"I need your help with something."

"Why do you need *my* help?"

"Talk to your grandmother, Sabina," Lizzie suggested and she began to appear a little transparent.

I blinked. "My grandmother?"

"Sabina will explain it to you," Lizzie said.

"Wait!" I said, as she faded away before my eyes.

"I'll be back." I heard her say, and then she

was gone.

I stood there shaking in reaction. My stomach was roiling, and my breath sounded loud to my own ears. I flinched hard when the phone on my desk began to ring. I ignored it and staggered to my chair. I plopped down, braced my elbows on the desk, and rested my face in my hands. As a precaution, I pulled the wastebasket out, in case my stomach decided to reject my lunch.

I waited for the shaking to pass, and began to recite the order of the major arcana cards of the tarot. It always calmed me down. *The Fool, The Magician, The High Priestess...*

"Nilah?" Dorothy popped her head in my office.

I peeked at her through my fingers. "Yeah?" *The Empress, The Emperor, The Heirophant...*

"Oh, sweetie are you sick?" she asked.

I grabbed at the excuse like a lifeline. "Yes, I'm sick." It would get me out of the building quicker than anything else. "The stomach flu maybe. I need to go home."

With Dorothy hovering over me, I gathered my things and left the building a short time later. When Alicia saw me, she stepped back as though I might be contagious. Dorothy was made of sterner stuff however, and she led me straight out and to my car.

My head spun as we walked to the parking lot.

I gave a half-hearted wave to Old Joe as he fussed with the mounds of orange chrysanthemums at the edge of the parking lot.

"Who are you waving at?" Dorothy wanted to know.

"At Old Joe the gardener," I said, pointing.

Dorothy came to a screeching halt and I bumped solidly into her. "Old Joe?" she said. "You knew Jozeph?"

Old Joe tipped his cap at me and faded away—right in front of my eyes... *Exactly as Lizzie had up in my office.* My knees started to tremble, and I could hear my pulse pounding in my ears. *What in the world was happening?*

"Sweetie, maybe I *should* drive you home. Jozeph Serafin, the former gardener, he passed away three months ago."

At her words, I dropped my car keys. "That can't be right. I've been speaking to him every morning for the past two months!"

Dorothy scooped up my keys and gently laid the back of her hand against my face, as if checking for a fever. "You do feel a little warm."

I was steered to my car and I blindly opened the door, and sat inside. "Okay," I said inanely. "Okay, I'll take myself home and get some rest."

Dorothy frowned but waved me off. "Sweetie, you go home, push the fluids, and take it easy."

I thanked her for her concern, started up my

car and backed out of the parking space. My mind focused on only one thing; speaking to my grandmother as soon as possible.

My mind was in chaos, yet I drove across town cautiously. *Jozeph Serafin, or Old Joe as he'd told me to call him—had been dead for the past three months? But I'd seen him almost every morning, and I'd talked to him...*

I braked hard at a stoplight. "But you never touched him, did you?" Saying the words out loud had a cold sweat running down my back. I recalled the feeling of my hand passing straight through Lizzie, and my stomach began to pitch, again. "Oh shit," I whispered.

A car honked behind me. The light had changed to green. I pulled away from the intersection and managed to make the rest of the trip without getting sick. With relief, I pulled around back of the line of historic brick buildings, one block away from the town square, where my grandmother worked; and we both lived.

Once I parked my car, I grabbed my things, and began to walk down the little brick path, ignoring the beautiful fall foliage that gave a sense of privacy to our small brick courtyard. Instead of taking the wood stairs with the ornate metal trim all the way up to my third floor apartment, I stopped at the little covered landing on the street level. I held onto the porch post, shut my eyes and tried to calm myself down.

The Lovers, The Chariot, Strength... I recited and thought hard on the image of the *Strength* tarot card that featured a woman holding a lion calmly in her arms. *Stay calm, be strong,* I told myself. I blew out a long cleansing breath and opened my eyes. Satisfied that I had myself under some semblance of control, I ducked under the colorful glass hanging lanterns that decorated the tiny porch and let myself straight into the back of the shop.

I shut the door behind me softly, as I wasn't sure if my grandmother was doing any readings this afternoon. Not disturbing a client had been ingrained in me since I'd been a child. Ahead of me a heavy, crimson brocade curtain blocked my view of the reading parlor, and I nudged the curtain aside to see if a reading was in progress.

Madame Sabina, sat alone in an ornately carved chair with her eyes closed. In front of her, tarot cards were artfully fanned out on a gorgeous antique round table. A crystal ball rested on a golden stand at her elbow and incense smoke wafted towards the ceiling. The room around her was decorated in shades of burgundy, and old gold, in sort of a gothic mish-mash of styles that clients and tourists expected and somewhere between a classy Gypsy *vardo*—

wagon, and an elegant Victorian séance room.

The brick walls of the room were hung with more brocade and tasseled curtains. Old vintage circus prints advertising fortune tellers and psychics decorated the walls in heavy gilt frames. The furniture was dark wood, the rugs were layered and antiques. A leather sofa ran along one wall and plush pillows in jewel tones and sumptuous textures abounded.

A cluster of LED candles "flickered" away on an ornate hutch, and behind the glass fronted doors, there were more crystal balls on stands. A few antique decks of tarot cards and old books on psychic development were displayed there as well. The reading parlor was dramatic, moody, mysterious and theatrical.

As was the woman who spoke without opening her eyes. "You come seeking knowledge?" she said, in a deep, heavily accented voice.

CHAPTER THREE

"It's me, *babcia,*" I used the Polish word for grandmother.

My grandmother sat draped in a turquoise colored, fringed shawl at the reading table. Her silver, curly hair was pulled back from her face and secured behind her head with a sparkly clip. Even in her seventies she was a striking woman. "Madame Sabina sees all and knows all..." she said dramatically.

I rolled my eyes at my grandmother's dry humor, and pulled the curtain closed behind me. "Yeah, yeah. Save it for the tourists."

"You should have some respect," she said. "And don't you roll your eyes at me *wnuczka.*"

Uh, oh, I thought. *She was dropping Polish words again.* Wnuczka—was Polish for granddaughter.

Whenever she called me that, it was a sure fire clue that she was peeved. "Sorry. I need to talk to you. Privately." I went directly to her. "This is important. Are you between clients?"

"I am. With your mother out of town, I have Vanessa out front watching the gift shop." Her eyes narrowed, as she focused on me. "What is wrong? There are very loud and distressed vibrations coming from you."

"That's probably because I think I'm losing my mind, and if not—well then I'm really going to start freaking out."

"Nilah, what is it?"

I stalked to the door that separated the reading parlor from the gift shop. "Hang on a sec," I said to my grandmother, then I opened it and poked my head in the store. "Vanessa," I called to get my sister's attention.

My younger sister sat behind the counter. Even at six months into her pregnancy, she was gorgeous—and she knew it. A stylish amber colored, maxi-dress draped over Vanessa's pregnant belly. She'd woven a colorful silk scarf through the mass of her hair that curled in golden-brown ropes to her waist. It was as if she'd come straight from a Coachella photo shoot.

Her chocolate brown eyes popped wide at my entrance. "What are you doing here at this time of day?" She stood and moved out from behind the counter.

"Long story. Would you—"

"Nilah," Vanessa cut me off and raised her eyebrows. She deliberately gave my black suit the once over. "That outfit isn't flattering on you. Not at all."

"We can't all dress like a Gypsy Princess. Some of us have to work real jobs." As soon as the snarky words left my mouth I regretted them. I blew out a breath and tried again. "Sorry. I'm dealing with something, and I need to talk privately to *Babcia*."

Vanessa tossed her head sending her chandelier style earrings swaying. "You could've just asked. Politely."

My nerves were shot, and I was running out of patience. I gripped the door handle and told myself to keep it together. "*Please*, make sure we aren't disturbed," I said through clenched teeth.

Vanessa checked the wall clock. "Madame Sabina's next appointment is at two o'clock. You've got twenty minutes."

"Your generosity never ceases to amaze me."

Vanessa planted her hands on her hips. "You've *always* been jealous of me."

I sighed. "I don't have time for an argument, Vanessa. This once, would you please help me out?"

"Fine." Vanessa turned her back on me in dismissal, and smiled at a trio of customers who'd entered the shop.

I ducked back into the reading parlor and locked the door behind me. I sat at the table, directly across from my grandmother. "I really do need your help."

She raised an eyebrow. "Must you two always snipe at each other?"

"Apparently." Unsure of what to do with my hands, I fidgeted for a moment and then clenched them together on the tabletop.

Grandma Sabina was an expert at reading people their faces and body language. She reached for my hands. "Tell me what is wrong."

"Some really weird things that have been happening to me at work... Especially today."

She leaned closer across the table, and her dark eyes locked on mine. "Yes?"

"I think I saw and spoke to someone who was *dead.*" When she didn't even flinch at that, I rushed to explain. "I saw a woman at the front desk. Then I saw her *in* her casket, and a few moments later she appeared upstairs *in my office.* She said she wanted me to help her...and then she—Lizzie the ghost—said that you would explain it all to me..." I waved my hands on either side of my head. "I know it sounds crazy!"

"Nilah," she said. "Slow down."

But I couldn't. As if saying what I thought out loud was the catalyst, my words tumbled one after another. Faster and faster. "Then there's the gardener, Old Joe. I've been *seeing* him for *two months*! And I've talked to him almost every morning...but they said he'd died three months ago—" I stopped rambling when my grandmother clamped her hand down on mine, hard.

"Start over. From the beginning," she said, sitting slowly back in her chair. "Tell me everything." Her eyes never left my face. "Take your time. Leave nothing out."

I took a breath, trying to compose myself. I started with meeting and talking to Old Joe, and as clearly as possible, explained everything that I'd experienced, including today. When I finished I clasped my hands nervously in my lap. "So, what do you think?"

Grandma Sabina's brow was lowered, her mouth set in a firm line. "You've seen and have communicated with spirits? More than once?"

I rubbed my forehead. "Yeah, it seems that I have." I dropped my face in my hands with a groan. "Ghosts. I've been seeing and talking to ghosts. This is freaking me out *Babcia*."

"And this all started since you began working at the funeral home?" Her words were slow and deliberate.

I snapped my head up, and considered her. "Yes, I suppose it did."

A huge blood-red amber ring in a silver setting seemed to glow on her hand as she tapped the cards fanned out on the table before her. "Choose a card."

I didn't argue. Grandma Sabina did nothing without a good reason. I passed my right hand palm-side down over the fanned out tarot cards. I felt a tug at my midsection, and it had me frowning. *That had never happened to me before.* I kept going but felt pulled back to where I'd felt that little inner nudge. I stopped over the area where the sensation intensified, and pulled the card out that seemed to be causing the reaction.

I flipped over the card and stared down at the image of a pretty young woman all in blue surrounded by splashing waves and holding an ornate cup. The girl in the card had a surprised expression on her face, but was smiling down at a large golden-orange fish that had risen up out of the cup, as if to share a secret with her.

"It's the *Page of Cups*," I whispered. "This tarot card represents a student or the discovery of psychic ability..." I trailed off as the implication set in.

"At last, Nilah," my grandmother said, searching my eyes. "You are *finally* coming into your gifts."

My stomach roiled and I swallowed back a feeling of dread. "I think I'm going to throw up."

"Bah!" She waved that away. "No you won't. That's simply your body reacting to what your subconscious already knows." She leaned forward and patted my hand. "I should have foreseen this. Your grandfather's mother had this particular..." she trailed off.

"Particular *what?*" My voice went up.

Her lips quivered into a sad little smile. "Gift," she finally decided.

That didn't sound good. I wet my lips against a mouth that had suddenly gone dry. "What particular gift?" I squeaked out.

"It would seem that you are *psychiczna średniej*."

I stared at her, and tried to translate the unfamiliar combination of words. *Psychiczna* that mean 'psychic' but the rest... "Shred-knee?" I tried to sound it out. "I don't know that word."

"*Psychiczna średniej*," she repeated. "A Medium. A Psychic-Medium."

I shook my head in denial. "Aw hell, no!"

"Nilah, you're very pale," she said soothingly. "Breathe deep, find your center, and calm yourself."

I pressed my hands to my stomach and made an effort to do as I was told. "What do I do now?"

"The tarot will show us. Pull two more cards,"

she said sliding the *Page of Cups* off to the side. "This time use your receptive hand."

"So I can receive impressions more clearly." I nodded and reached across the table towards the fanned out cards. The atmosphere in the reading room felt heavy and expectant. My left hand shook as I passed it over the cards once more. This time my hand stopped at two different points. I tapped the first card, my grandmother slid it free, and then I chose a second.

Grandma Sabina turned a tarot card over and what I saw had me cringing. The card showed a large red heart, pierced with three swords. The sky behind it was cloudy and gave the impression of rain—or tears—falling from the sky. "The *Three of Swords*." Her voice was neutral.

Even though I was a wash at performing readings for the general public, I still knew the basic definitions of every single card in the tarot deck. "Tears, delay and suffering." My voice sounded thick to my own ears.

Grandma Sabina turned the next card. It was a Major Arcana card. "*The Hanged Man*," she announced.

I gulped hard as I studied the image of a blonde, young man dangling upside down by his ankle, from a T-shaped living tree. The young man's expression was calm, almost peaceful, and a halo of light shone around his head. I shifted my gaze away from the card and into my grandmother's eyes. "A life in transition?"

"Yes." She nodded, confirming my words. "That is the elementary meaning... but you need to look deeper at the cards."

"Tell me."

"The *Three of Swords*, in this case illustrates that you have suffered in the past, believing that you had no abilities. However, your talents have simply emerged later in life. That is the *delay* the card is showing us here. Also, this card is a notice from Spirit that there is something yet to be learned."

I eyeballed that card and thought back to all the times I had cried, miserable as a teen over my apparent lack of skill. No matter how hard I had tried, my pretty little sister had performed circles around me. Even my older brothers Nicolas and Vincent had more ability. I cleared my throat against the emotions that the reading was calling to the surface. "And the deeper meaning of *The Hanged Man*?"

"You can achieve freedom by understanding and accepting the forces that are bringing about the change in your world. Do not fight these forces, *embrace* them. Do not be afraid of the visitations you have had—and are yet to receive. Try and help them. It is your destiny."

"Visitations? Destiny?" I sputtered. "This is

freaky stuff, *Babcia*. What if I don't want this destiny?"

Grandma Sabina held up *The Hanged Man* card to eye level. "If this card would have been drawn from the deck in a reversed position, then I would say you are fighting yourself, and denying who you are."

"But it wasn't," I said trying to follow where she was headed.

"Exactly." She gave a satisfied nod. "You are merely afraid right now... Startled at the discovery. But I want you to consider, that both of the spirits you have interacted with were good and kind to you."

"Lizzie was a little grumpy... she scared the crap outta me *materializing* in my office like that. But I guess you're right." I thought it over. "She wasn't mean. I never thought of it that way."

Grandma Sabina arranged the three chosen cards on the table in front of me. "The *Page of Cups* announces the discovery of a psychic talent. The *Three of Swords* is showing that you will not have an easy path to travel—and I'm sorry about that sweetheart." She gave my hand a little pat. "Finally, *The Hanged Man* shows that your life is in transition."

"Wow," I managed.

"Make no mistake," she said. "This is an initiatory phase of your life."

Overwhelmed, I turned my hand over and gripped hers. "Thank you, *Babcia*."

A discreet knock sounded on the door. "Sorry to interrupt," Vanessa called through the door. "Your two o'clock appointment is here."

"Thank you, I'll be right out," Grandma Sabina called back.

I stood up too fast, and my chair fell over with a little crash. "I'll clear out and let you get back to your clients." My voice broke on the words. I snagged the chair, righted it, and turned blindly for the exit.

A soft hand on my arm had me stopping in my tracks. "Stop, be calm."

I froze in place and closed my eyes. "I'm trying," I whispered.

"*Kochanie,* nothing happens in this life by chance."

Darling, she'd called me, and though her voice had been no-nonsense, the endearment had tears welling in my eyes. "Right," I managed.

"Know that I am here for you." She ran a hand down my hair. "I'll help you in any way that I can."

Behind us the doorknob rattled, I heard the lock flip, and the door to the reading parlor swung open. I swiped at my tears, and glanced back to see Vanessa staring at us with her mouth open. "What's wrong? What did you do?" my sister demanded of me.

"She did nothing!" Grandma Sabina spun on Vanessa. "Go out and shut the door behind you. Now!"

Vanessa goggled at our grandmother's unaccustomed harsh tone. "But...but your appointment is here."

Grandma Sabina marched across the parlor and nudged Vanessa out. "Tell them I will be out in five minutes," she said, shutting the door firmly in my sister's face.

A half-laugh escaped me at my grandmother's maneuver. "I can't believe you did that."

"Your sister is very demanding during her pregnancy. Sometimes I am tired of her..."

"Drama?" I suggested.

"I was thinking 'need for attention,' but, yes—I tire of her drama." Grandma Sabina reached up and framed my face with her hands. "Go. Rest, and clear your mind. We can speak more later."

Everything had changed. I realized, and found myself struggling against more tears. "I'm going to go up to my apartment. Think things over...take a nap maybe."

"Come down for dinner tonight," she invited. "I've got a meal in the crockpot."

"Sure, that sounds great." I said. "Thanks *Babcia.*" I ducked under the curtain, grabbed my bag and went out the back door. I climbed up the back stairs to the third floor of our building, stopping on the tiny covered landing right outside my door. I unlocked it, stepped inside and sighed in relief at being inside my own personal oasis of texture and color.

Squash, my orange tabby cat was waiting on the bright blue area rug inside the door. He dropped a cat toy at my feet and meowed. I gave the squishy, sparkly ball a gentle kick and it shot into the living room. He took off after it with a vengeance.

I tossed my keys in a Blue Willow bowl on my painted entryway table and set my purse next to it. Kicking my shoes under the narrow table, I headed directly for my bedroom. I stripped off my clothes and chucked them towards the hamper in the corner.

Only the blouse actually made it into the hamper.

I tugged back the comforter from my wrought iron bed and dove in. I flung my arm over my eyes and grunted when Squash walked up my body and sat on my chest. As a symbol of his love, he dropped the cat toy he was carrying on my face.

I picked up the toy, a green felt fish this time. "Not now, Squash."

Squash batted at my nose with a paw and leaned down to peer in my face. I rubbed his ears and he relented. The cat settled in with a loud purr and I drifted off.

CHAPTER FOUR

I woke up a few hours later with the groggy, thickheaded feeling that afternoon naps always gave me. I discovered that Squash had made himself at home sprawling cross-wise across my bed with his head propped up against my hip. As soon as I stirred, he rose and started digging around on the bed for his toy. The normality of it comforted me.

After a few seconds of searching, I found the felt fish. "You want this?" I asked him. As an answer, the tabby's butt lowered and began to wiggle back and forth in excitement.

"Go get it!" I tossed the toy and Squash dove off my bed and landed with a loud thud as he chased the toy.

I staggered out of bed and headed for the

kitchen. I put some water on for tea and stood yawning at the little kitchen sink. I squinted at the clock on the microwave. It was 4:55 and that meant Grandma Sabina would close the shop in precisely five minutes and serve her dinner at 5:30. If I wanted to mooch a meal, I needed to get my ass in gear. I smirked at myself, standing there in my lace violet colored bra and matching panties. *And, I should put some clothes on, too.* I thought.

I tossed a few more toys from Squash's impressive collection, and he happily romped around the apartment chasing and fetching—not unlike a dog. While I waited for the kettle to boil, I pulled on a pair of denim leggings, and a paisley, bohemian style top in shades of burnt orange and red. I took the chignon down and shook my hair out. After a quick dash back to the kitchen to pour the water over the tea leaves, I brushed out my hair and repaired my makeup.

By the time my tea had steeped, I was sitting at the little drop side table between the kitchen and living area, and I was starting to feel more like myself. Squash was bouncing from my sofa to the coffee table, and then rolling around on the rug, "killing" his favorite felt fish.

I ran my fingers over the kitchen table's distressed turquoise paint and considered what had happened today. So far everything 'Medium related' had happened at work. And I was determined to keep it that way. *I should probably talk to my grandmother about that,* I thought. At least I felt "safe" here in my apartment. It was bright and colorful with a Boho vibe, miles away from the demure, pastel walls of the Fogg Funeral Home.

A crazy quilt in velvets, satin and cotton fabrics draped over my second hand sofa. The cover was a mish mash of paisley, stripes and solids, with lots of blue and turquoise colors. I'd tossed two fat and fuzzy leopard print pillows on the sofa too for fun and texture. It was lush, sexy and relaxed. Instead of a lamp, colorful glass lanterns hung from the ceiling in different heights over one end table. Inside of the lanterns I used LED candles so I could have the flickering light without the fire hazard.

My end tables were rescued from garage sales and vintage shops. One table was painted in a bold red, and another had a sort of farmhouse style to it—with it's green painted legs and a slightly warped pine top.

Squash flipped his fish in the air and rolled under the coffee table, which had also seen better days. Another rescue, this was from my older brother Vincent's bachelor apartment. The table was chunky and the finish was scarred. I covered up the top with purple silk scarf, a mirror tiled tray that held fat candles, an antique set of tarot cards, and a stack of old books.

Squash lifted a tentative paw to bat at the fringe on the scarf that dangled over the edge of the table.

"Squash," I said in warning. The cat flipped his tail, to signal his annoyance, and took himself off to sit in the biggest window of my living room, along with my two light-up artificial pumpkins. He sat between them staring down at the street below, his fur matching the pumpkin's color almost exactly. Those pumpkins and an orange and purple strand of decorative lights clicked on, right on schedule, illuminating the large window. I had them set on a timer and I liked knowing their seasonal colors would be seen on the street outside, as well as adding some spooky, seasonal cheer to my apartment.

I heard a muffled chime and got up to dig my phone out of my purse. I narrowly avoided tripping on another cat toy as I sat on the sofa to check my text messages.

There were two from work. I propped up my bare feet on the table, wiggling my painted toes, as I scrolled through the texts. One was from Dorothy telling me to rest and that she hoped I felt better. The second was from Franklin Fogg, instructing me to notify him if I felt I would be unable to make it in to work tomorrow.

There was a message from my mother. She and my father were on an anniversary trip and she'd sent me several photos of the beach from Maine. I responded with a smiley face emoji and told them to have fun.

The last message was from my sister Vanessa. I made a face at my phone, seriously considered deleting the text, but went ahead and tapped on the screen anyway. It read: *I want to talk to you about today. ASAP. Call me.*

"Don't hold your breath, sis," I said, deleting the message.

Squash walked behind me, scaling the back of the sofa. He stopped and gave the back of my head a nudge with his. He'd never liked my sister, either.

I shook off the mood and went to grab a bottle of white wine from the iron rack on top of my fridge. "Want to go see Grandma?" I asked Squash. In answer the cat raced towards the kitchen door that led to the interior stairs.

I opened the door and Squash shot down the narrow stairwell. These were only used for family, as we all considered the outdoor stairs to be the main entrance. I went down more slowly than the cat, and stopped at Grandma Sabina's white painted door. I knocked and waited.

"Come in!" she called.

I opened the door and Squash strolled in

ahead of me. He was welcome in my grandmother's apartment as he got along with her two felines, Oscar and Ollie. Her apartment was laid out exactly as mine was. However, my grandmother's style of décor was very different. I'd always figured being surrounded by all of the burgundy and gold opulence in the reading parlor of the shop made her long for softer colors, and clean lines in her personal space.

The entire apartment was done in all muted gray, creamy white and with touches of blue. It was streamlined and calming. The furniture was white washed and had a slight beach vibe, and glass apothecary jars on her sofa table were filled with shells and cobbles from the nearby beach.

I shut the door, and followed my nose. "Whatever you're cooking smells great," I called out.

I found Grandma Sabina standing at her counter dishing up food into two heavy white bowls. "Chicken pot pie," she announced.

"I didn't know you could make that in a crock pot." I gave her a one armed hug.

"You can when your stove is broken," she said.

"Have you called a repairman?" I asked.

"I have. I expect him tomorrow."

"Well then, you really need this," I said waving the bottle of wine at her

My grandmother turned from the food with a smile. "Ah, you brought wine. Today, you are my favorite grandchild. Go ahead and open that, we will let this cool for a few minutes and then we will eat."

I went to a drawer and rooted around for the corkscrew. "I figured we could both use some wine after today."

I poured us each a glass and we sat at her kitchen table while the cats tumbled around in the pretty living room. At first, I kept the conversation on mundane things. We discussed my parents' trip, and I was brought up to speed on the latest town gossip. Finally I went ahead and asked about what had been bothering me.

I toyed with my wineglass. "So, I was wondering...you don't think that the ghosts I'm seeing at work will follow me back to my apartment, do you?"

Grandma Sabina brought the food to the table, sat and took her time before answering. "I believe that the visitations will be limited to the funeral home...for the time being."

"How's that?" I asked.

Grandma Sabina sat back and sipped her wine. "Think of the funeral home as a train station, if you will. Many spirits always coming and going."

I nodded and sampled the food. "So basically, I work in Grand Central Station for ghosts?"

Grandma Sabina chuckled. "That is a good way to visualize it. All those spirits of the recently departed are wandering around the station; trying to catch a train to their next destination."

"Okay, I can kind of see that."

"Now some know exactly where they need to go," she said. "But others..."

"Wander around, lost," I finished.

"Or they're too confused to understand what has happened. And so they need help, and they reach out to someone who is walking in both worlds for guidance."

I frowned. "Walking in both worlds? I don't understand."

"A Medium is like a bridge," My grandmother explained, as she poured each of us more wine. "They stand with a foot in both worlds—the world of spirit and the world of the living. A Medium acts as a sort of *link* between, making a connection and relaying messages back and forth."

"I think one of the first things Lizzie said to me was she wanted me to help her contact her family."

"I knew Elizabeth Samuel," my grandmother said casually.

"Wait, what?"

Grandma Sabina smiled at me. "She came to see me for readings once a year, like clockwork."

"She told me to come and talk to you," I said, considering the wine in my glass.

"And so you have."

I met my grandmother's eyes. "Lizzie said you would explain it to me."

"I have done my best. I only hope that I've helped you."

"So what do I do now? Go back to work and ask Old Joe and Lizzie what it is they want?"

"Exactly." Grandma Sabina nodded.

I set my spoon aside. "You make it sound so simple."

"*Kochanie*, I know very well that it is not," she sighed. "However, you have to embrace your destiny."

"I think of all the years I wished, hoped and prayed to have even a fraction of the talent you, Mama, and even Vanessa had."

"Be careful what you wish for," she said seriously.

I shuddered and tossed back what was left in my glass. "I think this calls for another bottle of wine."

***

The banging on the main door of my apartment was what woke me early the next morning. I rolled out of bed, groaned at the apparent wine hangover and staggered all the way to my door.

"I'm coming!" I yelled when the insistent knocking continued. Thinking it was one of my brothers being an ass, I didn't bother to check the spy hole and whipped the door wide open. "What?" I snarled.

The very brawny man that stood on my little apartment landing practically filled up the entire space. He had to have been at least six foot four, and I blinked up at him, estimating him to be in his early thirties. He wore a heavy leather jacket over a faded red flannel shirt. His long legs were covered in tough work pants, and the boots he wore had seen better days.

His hair was dark, and pulled back into a man bun. He had a striking, bearded face and warm brown eyes. His arched brows raised in surprise and then speculation, as he considered me.

I gulped and felt myself flush when I realized I was standing in front of him wearing my babydoll nightie that hit me mid-thigh. The all over floral lace was teal-blue, and I had a split second to think: *At least I was covered up...sort of.* The built in bra top was full coverage—but the rest of the lace was semi-sheer.

"Can I help you?" As soon as I said it, I flinched. *Probably not the best choice of words for the situation.*

He started to grin and then caught himself. Rubbing a hand over his chin, he cleared his throat instead. "Sabina Abram? You called about your stove?"

"No, that's my grandmother." I stood there and brazened it out. "She's one floor down."

"Ah." He stepped back. "I'll head downstairs, then."

I started to close the door. "I'm sure she's waiting."

"Sorry to disturb you," he said. To his credit he kept his expression bland. I didn't have to be psychic to know he was probably grinning the whole way down the steps.

I told myself not to overreact. Honestly, the man would've seen more skin if I'd bumped into him at the beach. But it was a bit embarrassing rolling out of bed in your nightie and opening the door to a guy who could pass for a romance-novel cover model.

Maybe he was an escapee from a nearby convention? The thought had me giggling and I went directly to the kitchen cabinet, took some acetaminophen, and started the water for tea— English Breakfast. I figured a morning like this called for a jolt of caffeine. I yawned and headed for the showers, wondering what that repairman would look like without his shirt on.

An hour later I was dressed for work, wearing the best of the worse of my uniform. A soft, pleated black skirt that was actually flattering and a scoop neck top in white. I shrugged my blazer on, gathered up my things and let myself out the door.

I'd only cleared the second floor landing, when my grandmother's door opened. I glanced over my shoulder and saw the repairman letting himself out. Determined not to feel embarrassed, I strolled down the stairs as casually as possible. I could feel him walking down the stairs, right behind me.

Once I hit the brick pavers of the courtyard, he fell into step with me. I nodded over at him as we walked towards the little parking area. "Hello again. What's the prognosis on the stove?"

He shifted his gaze over to me. "I'm ordering a part for Sabina. I should have it in a few days."

"That's good." I unlocked my car door and was surprised when he reached around to open the car door for me. "Um, thanks," I said, stepping back a bit.

"My pleasure." His deep voice rumbled as he stared down at me.

We stood there for a few moments with the car door between us. I had to look way up to meet his eyes. For the first time I was around a man who made me feel *small*. Usually I felt like a Valkyrie because of my curves, but this guy was built like a... *Barbarian*, I finally decided. *A big, brawny, sexy man-beast who would toss you over his shoulder and cart you off somewhere to do deliciously, naughty things to you.* My insides quivered at the unruly thought.

Clearly, I needed to get laid.

I did my best to cover my physical reaction. When he didn't make a move and continued to study me with a neutral expression, my curiosity got the better of me. "What?" I finally asked.

"You look like a banker in that outfit," he said, smiling. The brown of his eyes seemed to warm, and the transformation to his face had me catching my breath.

I broke eye contact first. "Ah, nope. Not a banker," I chuckled and tossed my purse in the car.

"Maybe I'm still back at that little teal number you answered the door in."

I slid my gaze back to his face, and decided the situation called for a little snark. "Sorry about that. Hopefully I haven't traumatized you for life."

"No." He threw his head back and laughed. "But you did make my day."

I couldn't help but smile in reaction. "Well, that's something, then." I climbed in my car.

"I'll see you around," he said, and closed the car door for me.

I watched him walk away. I made a mental note to talk to Grandma Sabina, because I definitely wanted to be around when he came back. Only this time, I'd shoot for a nice outfit and not my nightgown or frumpy funeral home uniform.

CHAPTER FIVE

I breezed into my office in an upbeat mood—
thanks to the flirtations of that sexy man-
beast of a repairman, *and* ready to face the world.
It certainly didn't hurt that there were no
sightings from Old Joe or Lizzie upon my arrival.

The burial for Elizabeth Sanders—Lizzie had
been scheduled for this morning at 10:30 am. So
when noon came and went and she didn't put in
an appearance, I breathed a sigh of relief and
assumed that she had moved along.

Caught her train so to speak.

Gone to the other side.

I leaned back in my chair and weighed my
options. Grandma Sabina had told me everything
she knew about Mediumship over dinner and
wine, and suggested that I do what I did best:

study and research. And I agreed. I definitely needed to read up on ghosts, hauntings and Mediumship ASAP if only to gain a better idea of what I was dealing with.

But who to contact and where to search?

There *were* Witches in Danvers, after all... Real ones. I thought about Tammy Pruitt the proprietor of the local magick shop. She carried lots of witchy supplies, *and* metaphysical books. She'd probably be able to point me in the right direction—reading material wise. I knew most of the shops ran extended hours through Halloween, and I decided to drop by the store after my shift ended and see what the staff suggested.

Satisfied with my plans, I turned my attention back to work. Everything was quiet on the third floor of the funeral home, and I decided to stay at my desk and eat lunch. I had only finished my turkey sandwich, when I discovered that Lizzie was standing, and gazing out the little round window in my office.

I froze in my chair for a moment, staring at the old woman's back. My heart pounded hard, but I forced myself to sit still and to calmly observe what was in front of my eyes. Sipping at my soda, I took in the scene. *Or would that be a sighting?*

I squinted at her form and could notice only a slight transparency to her image, even as the bright light streamed through the window and down upon her. At first I couldn't figure out why it seemed *off*, and then I understood. Her figure cast no shadow.

"You can squint at me all you want," Lizzie said. "I'm still here."

I jerked in my chair, quickly setting my soft drink down. "Well, I'm new to this. Cut a girl a break will ya?"

Lizzie turned and winked at me. "Got your sass back." She nodded in approval.

If this was truly going to be my path as my grandmother had said, then I needed to embrace it. So I decided then and there—to simply roll with it. "What can I do for you, Lizzie?"

Lizzie plopped her hands on her hips. "She took it. It didn't belong to her, but she took it anyway."

"Who took what?" I asked, standing and walking closer.

"My brooch." Lizzie hooked a thumb towards her chest and I noticed that the floral pin with the blue stone and pearls no longer appeared on her dress.

Despite myself, I leaned nearer. "Oh, no." I could see a slight tear in her jacket.

"That brooch was supposed to go to my only daughter, *not* my sister," Lizzie said. "Didn't I go to the trouble of hiring a lawyer and drawing up a will?"

"I'm sorry."

"Don't be sorry," Lizzie snapped. "And don't just stand there. Do something about it!"

"Maybe I better write this down," I heard myself say. "Gimme a sec." I scrambled for paper and pen while Lizzie paced the floor in front of me.

"Damned if she didn't take it anyway," Lizzie muttered. "Pulled it right off my jacket last night."

"So you're saying your own sister yanked the brooch off your jacket—here in the funeral home?" I asked, writing as quickly as possible.

Lizzie rolled her eyes. "That's what I said. Pay attention, girl."

"What's your sister's name?"

"Her name is Ethyl," Lizzie said. "Ethyl Marilyn Johnson."

"Ethyl?" I jotted the name down, but couldn't help making a face. "That's a horrible name."

"She always hated it. To this day she only uses her middle name. That trouble making, no good...*floozy*!" Lizzie shook her fist.

I glanced up from my notes. Her image was fading fast. "Umm, maybe you shouldn't excite yourself."

"Why the hell not?" Lizzie said. "It's not like it's going to kill me!"

"There's that," I said. "But it's like the more you rant and rave...the less 'here' you are."

"I guess getting wound up makes the etheric energy burn out faster," Lizzie said.

"The etheric what?" I shook my head in confusion. "How in the hell would you know something like that?"

"Actually, I watched ghost hunting shows with my granddaughter, Beth." Lizzie brushed at her sleeve. "I learned some of the lingo."

"Lingo," I repeated, and couldn't help but smile. *I was really starting to like this old lady.*

"Yeah, she says I'm one bad-ass granny." Lizzie's voice started to fade as well.

"Lizzie!" I said before her ghost disappeared. "Is there anything else I need to know?"

"Please fix this mess. Help my family...." and she was no longer in the room.

Now, alone in my office, I didn't want to forget anything important. I hustled back to my desk, going over my notes. "There was a tear in her jacket," I said. "Oh man, how was I able to *see* a tear in a jacket of a ghost?" I tapped my pen against the notepad as I considered it. "Maybe because she wanted me to see it?"

I shook my head and wrote down my impressions. "Good god, what sort of person steals the jewelry off a body in a casket?" I muttered, rubbing my forehead. "Ethyl the floozy apparently," I said, answering my own question.

For good measure I underlined the word 'floozy,' then added that the sister only used her middle name. In the margin on the page I added: *Lizzie watched ghost hunting shows with Beth. Beth calls her a bad-ass granny.*

I tore the page from my notepad and slipped it in my purse. I'd no sooner shut the desk drawer when Franklin Fogg burst in my office. "We have an emergency meeting. All staff in the conference room. Right now," he said.

Shocked at his grim tone, I jumped to my feet and followed him downstairs. Franklin stood at the door to the main conference room and held it open. I went in, took a seat and spotted Dorothy, several greeters, Alicia, Tommy and Joanne.

Franklin took the last empty chair. He bushed at his salt and pepper hair distractedly and fidgeted with his tie. He folded his hands on the tabletop and addressed the group. "Before the service at the funeral home chapel, Mrs. Samuels' jewelry was to be removed and given to her children, prior to her casket being sealed... Her pearl necklace, wedding rings and a brooch."

My heart began to race as Franklin spoke. *The brooch.* I gulped hard. I knew where this was going.

"The pearls and rings were accounted for, however the topaz and pearl brooch is missing," he said. "I personally searched for the brooch this morning after its loss was pointed out. We also moved the casket to a private room before the service, to remove the body and search through the lining of the casket. The jewelry was not found."

"We have contacted the police and our insurance company," Alicia piped in. "But Mrs. Samuels' children are distraught, and unless the brooch is discovered and returned, criminal charges are likely to be filed."

There was a knock and a uniformed police officer stepped into the conference room. "Hello," he said, closing the door behind him.

Alicia smirked at everyone who was assembled. "This is Officer Casper. If anyone has any information about the missing brooch, this would be the time to speak up." Clearly she was enjoying the drama of it all.

What could I say? I thought. *Nothing, unless I wanted to sound like a raving lunatic.* I closed my eyes and imagined how that would play out... *Oh excuse me Officer, the ghost of Elizabeth Samuels appeared to me upstairs in my office and told me that her 'floozy' of a sister tore the brooch right off her jacket while she lay in the coffin?*

I'd be fired in a heartbeat, even *if* they believed me. Afraid to say anything, I kept my mouth shut.

"I have a question," Tommy spoke up. "What about Mrs. Samuels' family? Has anyone questioned them in regards to the missing brooch?"

Yes! I thought, turning my head to check the police officer's expression.

"Yes, we have, and nothing has been ruled out."

An hour later after being questioned by the nice police officer, I was allowed to go back to my desk. He'd asked me about my being 'sick' yesterday, and what time I'd left. Fortunately for me, the brooch had still been in place when I'd left the building. I was also warned by Franklin not to discuss 'the situation', as he called it, with anyone outside of the office. If I did it would be grounds for immediate dismissal.

I sat staring at the last spot Lizzie had materialized in. "Lizzie?" I whispered to my empty office hoping for a response. There was none. After another half hour of waiting and expecting Lizzie to reappear, I gave up and grabbed a huge stack of folders from a nearby table. There was always filing to be done. Some of the folders had been there before I even started.

The funeral home really needed to hire an intern for full time filing, I thought. Shrugging it off, I headed off to the basement filing room, determined to find a way to fill the rest of my shift. I was on my way down to the storage/file room when I overheard Alicia and Franklin in the middle of a heated argument. I froze in mid-step.

"I'm telling you," Alicia hissed. "It's *her!*"

"That's enough, Alicia," Franklin attempted to soothe his wife.

"You can't trust a Gypsy!" Though her voice was hushed, the derision in it was plain. "I told you *not* to hire her."

Shocked at her statement I stayed where I was on the stairs and eavesdropped on the bigoted, bleached blonde, without a qualm.

"Stop it!" Franklin's voice was low but firm. "There is no reason to think that Nilah had anything to do with it,"

Thanks, boss. I thought, and released my breath slowly.

While Alicia continued to cast disparaging comments on my heritage, I eased back up a few steps, and then began to stomp in place a few times. I continued marching my way loudly down the stairs, humming the chorus of Cher's old hit, *Gyspies, Tramps and Thieves.*

I came around the corner of the stairs and stopped as if I was surprised to find them there. "Oh, excuse me," I said.

Alicia turned pale and then a rather alarming shade of red. She bolted past me without a word, brushing hard enough against me to knock several folders from the stack. They hit the floor with a splat.

Franklin knelt down immediately. "Let me help you," he said.

"Thanks," I said, studying him as he scooped up the folders. *What would posses such a nice guy to marry a woman like that? I bet the woman never even had an orgasm. She was totally the type that you'd picture filing her nails during sex.*

"Here you go," he said holding out the files.

I almost felt pity for the man. "Are you alright, Franklin?"

"Yes, I'm fine," he said, mouth tight and shoulders stiff. He placed the files carefully on top of the stack I was carrying—like he expected them to explode.

"I'll go...file these," I said with false cheer.

Franklin stepped back allowing me to pass. "Thank you, Nilah," he said, moving back again, ensuring that he wouldn't accidentally come into contact with me.

"Sure," I said, going straight for the file room. I closed the door behind me and placed the stack of files on top of the nearest file cabinet. I blew out a long breath, and told myself to stay calm, even as I played the scene over in my head. *Losing my temper wouldn't solve a thing.* I reminded myself, and picked up the top file. When I focused on the name, I nearly bobbled it.

The file read: Jozef A. Serafin.

This was Old Joe, the gardener's file. I opened it slowly. *Date of birth, 1945. Date of death... was only a few months ago.* I saw that Old Joe had passed away at his home, *and* that he was a Vietnam Veteran. "You were a decorated Marine to boot," I said in wonder. A military marker was in the process of being issued. I noted the dates of his funeral service, and of the date and place of his interment. The cemetery was a local one.

I read that the funeral arrangements had been made by his grandson—Mr. Joseph Serafin. "Was this the grandson you kept telling me I should meet?" I wondered.

"Find anything interesting in my file?"

I recoiled so hard I bounced off the filing cabinet. "Damn it!"

Sitting on top of a nearby cabinet, was Old Joe. "Sorry," the ghost said cheerfully.

I rapped my fist against my chest. "Between you and Lizzie I'm going to have a heart attack! Would you guys *stop* doing that?"

"Doing what?"

"Appearing!" I snapped. "Materializing... whatever."

"Well, it is almost Halloween," he said perfectly straight faced.

I frowned at him. "That's not funny."

"I wasn't trying to be funny. I meant that the veil between this world and the next is thin right now. It's easier for us to pop back and forth. To communicate."

"Oh." *Wasn't that interesting?* I studied the ghost where he perched on top of the file cabinet, swinging his feet. He was still wearing his gardener uniform. "Can I ask you a question?" I said cautiously.

"Sure."

"Why are you appearing to me wearing your gardening service outfit. Wouldn't you have been buried in your Marine dress uniform?"

Old Joe sighed. "I died wearing the gardening service uniform. I was out in my backyard weeding my vegetable garden and then..."

I held up a hand. "I'm sorry! I wasn't trying to upset you."

"I did two tours of Vietnam. It takes a lot more than talking about how I kicked off in the vegetable garden to upset me."

"Then why are you here?" I asked.

"You need to meet my grandson," Old Joe said. "I'm starting to get a little frustrated with all the waiting."

My mouth hit the floor. "So you came from the other side to play matchmaker?"

"That, and so you'd have a chance to get used to the spirits that will be coming to you for help."

Old Joe floated down from the filing cabinet and moved closer.

"You tricked me," I reminded him. "I thought you were a—well, a living person for months."

"I only wanted to help you. Also, I wanted to ask if you'd give my grandson a message for me?"

"Your grandson? He'd think I was bat-shit crazy if I told him his grandfather had a message from the other side." I pointed out.

"No, he wouldn't," Old Joe insisted. "Trust me."

I inspected the file I still held in my hand. His grandson, Joseph Serafin had made all of the funeral arrangements. "The contact information should be in your file. It wouldn't be difficult to track him down for you."

The ghost tossed back his head and laughed. "*Kochanie*, you've already met him."

"I have?" I asked. "When?"

"Recently," he said wheezing with laughter.

"For god's sake!" I tossed up my hands. "Be cryptic, why don't you?"

"Well, that *does* make this a little more fun." Old Joe grinned.

I rolled my eyes. "Fine. What's the message?"

"Tell him that I love him, and that I'm proud of him. Also, I left a little something extra for him in the garden shed." Old Joe's image began to fade.

"You love him. You're proud of him. The garden shed," I repeated. "What is it he's supposed to find?"

The ghost of Old Joe reached out and I felt a gentle pressure on my shoulder. Almost as if his hand rested there. "The white rose," he said, and vanished.

Alone in the suddenly ice cold file room, I shuddered.

CHAPTER SIX

I stood on the sidewalk, staring up at a massive sign that was suspended over the front door of the local magickal shop. A crescent moon smiled down and golden stars were scattered across the signage. I stepped nearer and peered through the window, checking the place out before I entered. They were doing a booming business this evening. The interior brick walls were high and filled with chunky shelves that held an amazing amount of goods. I could see racks for handmade soaps and lotions, shelves of books and accessories, a display of handmade brooms, and a large table filled with glass bowls of colorful tumbled stones.

I didn't see Tammy, but a goth-looking employee with burgundy hair stood behind the carved wood front counter, next to a cool antique cash register, chatting with a group of women. I eased back from the doorway when another trio of women strolled out wearing long dresses and dark, jewel tone velvet capes. As one, the trio pulled the hoods up over their hair and they strolled off down the sidewalk without a care in the world, chatting amongst themselves.

One of them was carrying a long carved broomstick.

And people accused the Roma of being flashy. I shook off the snide thought and psyched myself up. Taking a deep breath, I pulled my hair out of the bun I'd tried to tame it into for work, shook out my hair, and entered the shop.

The employee made eye contact and strolled over to me. "Hi, I'm Christy. Can I help you?" She wore a black lacy top and a large silver pentagram sparkled against it. In direct contrast to the occult jewelry and dark eye makeup, her voice was bright and sunny, which tamped down on my anxiety somewhat.

I smiled. "Hi."

"Hey, you're Nilah Stephanik. Sabina Abrams granddaughter, right?"

"Yes, I am," I said, tugging on my funeral home blazer. I'd forgotten about the stupid employee name tag on my lapel. "I was searching for a book on a specific topic. And wondered if you'd be able to recommend a good one?"

Christy gestured over to the book racks. "Which topic?"

I fumbled over the possible double entendre. "Witch?"

Christy's blue eyes danced. "What sort of book are you shopping for, Nilah?"

"Oh," I laughed a little self-consciously. "Well, what I'm looking for might sound a little unusual."

"Don't worry." She flashed a conspirator's grin. "I can handle it."

I moved farther away from a group of shoppers. "I'm trying to find books on..." I lowered my voice. "Mediumship and spirit communication."

Christy didn't even blink. "Sure thing," she said. "Follow me."

I trailed along behind her as she went straight to her book section and pulled several books off the shelf. "The store is really great," I said, trying to act casual. "I especially love those handmade brooms that are on display." I pointed to the brooms arranged bristle end up, on the brick wall.

"Thanks." She smiled at me from over her shoulder. "The ceremonial brooms are popular sellers, especially close to Samhain."

"Samhain is the old Celtic name for the

modern day festival of Halloween, right?"

"Exactly. It's the Witches' New Year," she explained. "So, are there any other metaphysical topics you're interested in?" she asked.

"Well now that you mention it..." I checked again, making sure no one was close enough to overhear me. "Ghosts and hauntings."

Christy pulled a couple more books and motioned for me to follow her. She stopped outside of a curtained off reading room. "Why don't you sit in here, have a quick look-see and figure out which book would best suit your needs?"

"That'd be great!" I said, feeling relieved and took a seat at the reading table.

"If you need anything, wave me over." Christy plopped the books down. "Any books you don't want, you can leave here on the table."

I smiled up at her. "Thanks Christy."

I spent the next little while paging through the books. One was on a wide variety of psychic topics. It seemed promising and very down to earth. I read through the introduction and found myself laughing over the author's sense of humor. I set the book aside, patting the cover. *This one's a keeper.* The other books on Mediumship didn't resonate with me. So I stacked them up and out of the way.

The books on ghosts were very interesting.

After thumbing through them, I decided to buy both of them. I gathered my selection and rose, and headed to Christy who was once again, behind the checkout counter.

To my disappointment Christy didn't ring me up on the antique cash register. She began to use a touchscreen point of purchase program on an iPad that was mounted on a stand. "Find what you were hunting for?" she asked, flipping her wine-red hair over her shoulder.

I nodded. "Yes, I think I did. Thanks for your help."

Christy totaled up my purchases. "No problem."

I handed her my debit card. "I figured this would be the best place to come for information on ghosts and such."

"Why's that?" Christy asked, swiping the card through the reader.

"Well, you know…" I said, checking to make sure our conversation was still private. "You're *obviously* a Witch." I nodded towards her pentagram. "So I assumed you'd be the one to ask."

Christy threw back her head and laughed. "Just because I'm a Witch doesn't mean I'm an expert on ghosts and hauntings."

"Oh," I said, feeling like a moron.

Christy grinned at me. "Honey, it's not like

ghosts and Witches hang out on the weekends and swap recipes."

I couldn't help but grin in response to her good natured humor. "Yeah, I see your point. That would be like assuming that all *Roma* live in a *vardo*."

Christy tucked her tongue firmly in her cheek. "But those wagons are so colorful and pretty."

"So long as you're not claustrophobic."

"I'm glad you came in," Christy chuckled, and handed me back my card and the receipt.

"Me too." I plucked a pen out of a holder on the counter and signed my name. After Christy tucked the books in a bag, I handed her back the receipt.

"Drop by anytime," Christy said and slid the bag across the counter.

"Thanks, I will."

"Hi, handsome!" Christy beamed at someone over my shoulder. "I've got your soap order right here."

I felt someone move up from my right and I stepped over for the other customer. I glanced over and discovered none other than that sexy man-beast of a repairman.

"Hi Christy," he said, stepping up to the counter. When he saw me, his lips turned up.

I returned his smile. "Hi there."

Christy turned and picked up a gift bag with

twisted paper handles from the rear counter. The brown bag was tied up with a raffia bow. It was artsy and earthy all at the same time. She set the bag on the counter between us. "Here you go."

I could smell the soap from where I stood. It was spicy and had hints of patchouli. It made me think of the forest, and campfires. It suited him. Then I focused on the name written neatly in black marker on the bag: Joseph Serafin.

Holy shit! Old Joe had said that I'd already met his grandson. I flinched a bit and tried to cover my reaction. "You're Joseph Serafin?"

He turned to me slightly. "I am."

"I've met your grandfather."

"You knew him?"

"I do—did," I corrected myself.

He narrowed his eyes at the work uniform. "You work at Fogg Funeral Home?"

I picked up the bag of books. "Yes."

"I don't recall seeing you at the funeral."

Time to go. I ignored his comment and nodded to Christy. "Thanks, Christy." I turned and quickly left the shop before I could say anything to embarrass myself further.

Clutching the bag to my chest, I had to force myself to walk and not run down the crowded sidewalk. It was a short walk to my building, but it took longer than I expected. Tourists and locals were out in droves this evening, enjoying the

Halloween lights, cornstalks and pumpkins displayed on the square.

I had to navigate my way through a large group of women all wearing Halloween t-shirts. The group was admiring the orange, purple and green lights wrapped around the trees, and were chatting to each other.

"Excuse me, Miss?" I heard a woman call out.

The next thing I knew I found myself holding a friendly tourist's camera and taking a few pictures of her group as they posed by a large autumn display. It took a few moments, but the group was so cheerful that it made me laugh as the women mugged for the camera.

Finally they were done, and when they informed me that they were in town for a few more days I suggested they drop by Madam Sabina's for a tarot reading. Being a dutiful granddaughter I passed out my grandmother's business cards, and waved farewell and turned towards home.

"Nilah!" A deep male voice called from behind me.

I stopped and checked over my shoulder. Joseph Serafin was walking straight towards me. *Wow,* I thought. *Old Joe's grandson was a prime specimen.* Then I flushed, feeling slightly appalled at my rampaging hormonal reaction. I cleared my throat. "Oh, hey," I said, trying to play it cool.

"Arc you headed home?" he asked.

"I am." The fact that I managed not to stammer in response had to be a good sign.

He towered over me, all beefcake and brawn. "Want some company on your walk?"

Woof. No red-blooded female would turn that down. "Sure." I said, barely resisting the urge to jump up and cheer... Or to throw myself at him.

Nice night," Joseph said as we walked along.

"It is," I replied, wondering again at the sheer bulk of him. He moved well, confidently. It was a novel experience for me spending time with a man who made me feel uber feminine. Then again, he was very much the alpha male. *Probably would be best not to imagine what he'd be like in bed...* I shook my head and tried to focus on the task at hand. If I wanted to talk to him about his grandfather—I needed to pull myself together.

Fortunately Joseph seemed unaware of my inner struggle. Otherwise, I doubted he would be walking along so casually.

"So you knew my grandfather?" he said.

"I do."

Joseph frowned over the present tense as opposed to the past. "You mean you *did*."

I took a deep breath and steeled myself for what was to come. "No, I meant I *do*. Know him that is."

Joseph's eyebrows lowered. "Are you making a

joke?"

"Okay, here's the thing..." Running a hand through my hair, I took the plunge. "You know how in my family there are a lot of fortune tellers—psychics?"

"Yes. Everybody in town knows that." He shrugged. "Your grandmother, mom and sister all do readings at Sabina's shop..." He met my eyes. "Except for you."

"That's right because I've never had a knack for it. It's not my gift. I don't foresee the future..." I paced away a few steps, turned and strode back. "I have zero talent for divination of any kind. But it turns out that I got something else instead."

Joseph crossed his arms over his massive chest. "Meaning what?"

"I guess that I'm a Medium. I can communicate with the dead. Sort of."

"Excuse me?" He seemed suspicious, and scowled at my words.

"Honestly, this was news to me too!" I said. "I met your grandfather on my first day at Fogg Funeral Home back in August. He introduced himself to me as Old Joe."

"My grandfather died in July," Joseph said through his teeth and started to walk away.

I followed after him. "But I didn't know that! I saw Old Joe almost every day out in front of the building tending to the flowers. We talked and he'd asked about my *babcia*... And your grandfather kept telling me that I should meet you."

"That's not funny." Joseph shook his head, plainly not believing me.

"I am *not* joking," I assured him. My mind raced as I tried to come up with something to say, something to make him believe me. I put my hand on Joseph's arm and he stopped on the sidewalk, studying me intently.

"Describe him to me," he said.

"He told me that he died working in his vegetable garden, and that he had done two tours of Vietnam."

Joseph took a few steps farther away. "Anybody could have told you that," he said.

I let my hand fall to my side. "Your grandfather likes to toss phrases at me in Polish, and it always has me scrambling to translate... He still wears his gardener uniform and has this old beat up ball cap. He pulls it down too low. It makes his hair tuft out around his ears."

Joseph flinched. "Stop it."

For god sake! I thought. *I had royally screwed this up!* I took a deep breath and tried to make amends. "Joseph, I'm sorry that you don't believe me. This is new to me and I'm learning as I go. And if I upset or frightened you, I apologize."

Joseph rolled his eyes, but his shoulders seemed stiff. "You don't scare me."

"Pissed you off though," I said and he whipped his head around to glare at me. "You don't have to be a psychic to read facial expressions and body language." I shrugged.

We came to a stop at the little gate behind the shop. Joseph shoved it open so that the metal gate banged against a brick post. "Goodbye, Nilah," he said.

I walked through and watched Joseph stalk away. "Joseph?" I called after him.

He glanced back at me. "What?"

"Your grandfather loves you, and is so proud of you. He wanted you to know that."

Joseph stared at me for a long moment, then he walked off and disappeared into the darkness.

CHAPTER SEVEN

I went directly to my grandmother's apartment after Joseph Serafin had stalked off and told her about the drama at the funeral home, Lizzie, and the missing jewelry. After that I swallowed my pride and admitted everything that had happened while Joseph had walked me home.

Well okay, I left out my lustful fantasies of that sexy man-beast bending me over any available flat surface—I didn't think *that* would go over too well with my grandmother. God knows I couldn't decide whether I was delighted or horrified by my reaction to him. Not that it mattered now. The chances of him ever speaking to me again were nil.

However, I was honest about what a mess I'd made trying to tell Joseph about his grandfather.

And boy did *that* earn me a lecture on reader and client protocol.

"You grew up watching your mother and I perform readings!" It was Madame Sabina speaking—shouting at me now. She tossed up her hands and rattled off several colorful phrases in Polish. She abruptly switched back to English "Have you learned nothing?"

"Well, I—"

"You should have spent less time feeling sorry for yourself and *more* time paying attention!"

"Hey, this is all new to me—" I began and fell silent when my grandmother cut me off with *the look*. I winced in reaction. "Maybe you could give me a break." I muttered under my breath.

She walked across the room and reached up, cupping my face in her hands. "*Kochanie,* I am worried for you. And I am angry with myself for not seeing the signs sooner. It wasn't an accident that you ended up working at a funeral home."

"What?" I narrowed my eyes. "You mean it was fate that pushed me there?"

"I think that is exactly what happened." She leaned in closer, searching my eyes. "Yes, I see." She nodded at whatever she'd *seen*, and released me. "When one ignores their path... sometimes destiny takes control and shoves you in the direction you were meant to go."

"Or maybe I'm just really bad at this Medium

stuff."

"Bah!" She waved that away. "You are my granddaughter. You have mine and your grandfather's blood in your veins. I should have *known* what your gifts would be. I should have trained you myself instead of leaving you be as your mother insisted."

"Blaming yourself for my Rookie mistakes won't work *babcia*."

My grandmother frowned over that. After a few seconds, she nodded slowly. "Yes, this is true. Perhaps you and I are meant to learn this lesson together."

I took her hand. "Okay. I'm game if you are."

She pulled me into a tight hug. "*Kocham cię,*" she said—*I love you.*

I held on to her for a few moments, wondering how I had ever gotten so lucky as to have this woman in my life. I laid my head on her shoulder and sighed when I felt her hand pass over my hair. "Still," I said. "I've upset and frightened someone."

"Yes, you have, and that is never acceptable." My grandmother gave me a bolstering squeeze. "You must make reparation."

"I'll find a way," I promised.

After our talk, I went upstairs to my apartment and tried to sleep, but instead, I lay awake most of the night going over and over in my mind what I could have said differently, or done that wouldn't have been met with such derision and disbelief. I'd embarrassed myself. And I couldn't use the whole *"golly I didn't know any better,"* excuse ever again.

I pulled out my new books, a few highlighters and ink pens, and a legal pad for notes, and started studying. Squash stretched out at the end of my bed and kept a careful eye on my activities. It had been a while since I pulled an all nighter. But this situation definitely seemed to call for it.

The book on Mediumship and psychic abilities that I'd bought had pretty much the same thing to say about client and reader ethics as my grandmother had. The author firmly suggested ignoring reality television and the so called Mediums who dive bomb unsuspecting people on camera while their innocent targets were simply trying to go about their business.

Obviously, a reputable and ethical Psychic-Medium does *not* drop into casual conversation that they've been speaking to someone's dead relatives. Nor do they volunteer information when they are unsure of how it will be received.

I cringed even as I highlighted that particular section. In other words, I stopped and wrote down my thoughts on the legal pad: *If a person asks—you can tell them. If they don't—keep your mouth shut.*

I couldn't afford to make such a careless mistake again, especially with the situation at the funeral home and the missing brooch. If I wasn't careful, I'd find myself out of a job, or worse, under suspicion from the police. *Or* people in town would think I was bat-shit crazy.

Still, I learned quite a bit as I worked my way through my new books. When the sun came up, I rubbed my bleary eyes, started some tea and threw myself in the shower. Once I was finished, I wrapped myself in a plush raspberry colored towel, and found Squash sitting on top of my dresser, waiting for me.

I patted his head. "It's going to be one long-assed day Squash."

Squash made a feline mutter in agreement.

I started working the brush through my wet hair. "But I'm going to do better today. No more Rookie mistakes."

Squash vocalized his agreement with a long *Meow*.

***

I'd maybe been working in the third floor office of the funeral home for an hour before my first ghostly visitation of the day. I'd stopped to take a drink from my water bottle and...

"She's here!" Lizzie appeared beside me with no warning.

I'd been in mid swallow, and I choked,

coughed and sprayed water in her general direction.

Lizzie frowned at me. "It's a damn good thing I'm incorporeal, otherwise you'd have spit that water all over my dress."

I grabbed a tissue and blotted my chin and my own jacket. "Damn it!"

"That's not very lady like," Lizzie said as I thumped my chest and attempted to breathe.

I started to laugh and cough at the same time. "What isn't lady like? The choking or my spraying water all over the carpet?"

"Well pull yourself together," Lizzie said. "Because she's here!"

"Who's here?"

"My sister, the no-good, light fingered, *floozy*!"

"What's she doing here?"

"She came in with my family to talk to the police!" Lizzie swooped around my desk. "Hurry, get yourself downstairs!

Caught up in the moment, I jumped up and found myself hustling down the back stairs, with Lizzie leading the way. "Do you have a plan?" I whispered to her. "Because if this goes wrong, I'm going to lose my job and probably end up in the loony bin."

"The hell you will." Lizzie stopped at the bottom landing. She tossed me a grin over her shoulder. "Trust me."

I took a deep breath and stepped up beside her. "You'll stay with me?"

"Of course! I'm here to help *you* as much as you are to help me." Lizzie planted her hands on her hips. "I would've thought you'd have figured that out by now."

"They're in the conference room, I'll bet."

"Yes they are," Lizzie said. "My daughter Justine has been crying over this and *that* makes me angry. My Beth is there and she's trying to keep it together for her mother."

"Beth. She's the granddaughter you watched the ghost hunting television shows with," I said, remembering.

"That's right. She's about your age. You two would get along like a house afire." Lizzie nodded.

Knowing that Lizzie's daughter and granddaughter were distraught over the theft didn't sit well. It also made me a little angry—for Lizzie. "I suppose I could walk in and say someone contacted me, and that I have some information that could help."

Lizzie patted my arm. "There you go."

"Well, let's do this." I squared my shoulders, pushed the door open, and marched down the hall with Lizzie by my side.

"Let's give them one hell of a show." Lizzie rubbed her hands together.

"Oh my god." I tried not to laugh. "Behave yourself, woman," I whispered, and knocked briskly on the conference room door. I opened it without waiting for an answer.

We—Lizzie and I—entered the room and I shut the door. Six people were sitting around the big table. I saw that Franklin had served coffee and water. Glass tumblers with a Fogg Funeral home logo were sitting in front of the women of Lizzie's family. The policeman sipped at his coffee and I saw it was the same cop from the other day, Officer Casper. As one, they all stopped speaking and stared at me.

Franklin Fogg, frowned up at me. "Nilah? What is it?" He rested his hands on the papers in front of him.

I cleared my throat. "I believe I have some information about the missing brooch."

Officer Casper, narrowed his eyes at me. "What sort of information?"

"Recently, a source who wishes to remain anonymous, contacted me about the missing jewelry of Mrs. Samuel."

"Oh?" Alicia arched one penciled brow in disbelief.

Lizzie had her ghostly hand on my arm in support, and feeling brave, I focused on the elderly woman seated at the table. She was wearing a thick blue cardigan and a bored expression. "You're Mrs. Johnson, Elizabeth Samuel's sister, correct?"

"Yes," she said in a thin voice.

Lizzie leaned close to me, her voice sounded clearly in my ear. "Ask her if she was aware that the brooch was willed to Justine."

I nodded slightly in response to Lizzie's ghostly request. "Mrs. Johnson, were you aware that the brooch was willed to your sister's daughter, Justine?"

The old woman's lips pursed up and she turned her head away slightly, but she didn't respond.

Justine, an attractive woman, maybe in her sixties, swung her gaze to her aunt. "Aunt Marilyn? I don't understand. What's going on here?"

Beth rose to her feet. "Wait. How did you know about the will?" she asked. "What the hell is going on?"

Alicia began to complain at the lack of decorum, and Franklin stood. "If we could all please stay calm," he pleaded.

"I'm only trying to help," I said.

"Nilah, that's quite enough out of you!" Alicia said.

Officer Casper waved off Alicia. "Be quiet Mrs. Fogg," he said, in a no-nonsense tone of voice.

Alicia shrieked her outrage at the police officer, who ignored her. Justine was sobbing, and Beth was trying to comfort her mother, while Mrs. Johnson, sat with her arms crossed over her chest. Franklin desperately tried to get his wife to shut up, and the cop leaned back in his chair watching everyone and everything unfold with great interest.

"Nilah." Lizzie suddenly appeared across the room, waving at me from behind her sister's chair. "Ethyl is wearing the brooch right now." I could hear her plainly over the other voices. "It's pinned on a chain and it's under that hideous sweater," she told me.

"Okay, I'll tell them," I said. Then bit my lip as everyone gaped at me. A little embarrassed, I cleared my throat. "Is it possible that this was simply a misunderstanding about who the brooch was bequeathed to?" I said to Lizzie's sister as gently as possible.

The old woman tossed her head, regally. "Are you accusing me of something, young lady?"

"I'm not accusing you of anything. Ethyl," I said calmly.

There was a gasp of reaction over my use of the woman's first name. Before anyone could say anything, Ethyl's water glass was suddenly knocked over. Everyone jumped.

Justine shot to her feet. "How'd you know that

my Aunt Marilyn's first name is really Ethyl?"

I kept my expression bland even as Lizzie moved to stand closer to her daughter and granddaughter. "A friend told me," I said, and the lights above me began to flicker. *Wow, Lizzie's going all out,* I thought.

Beth rose up slowly, frowning at the overhead lights. "Is that *friend* here with us right now?"

I met Beth's eyes, the same blue as her grandmother's and smiled. "She is."

"I *knew* it!" Beth sounded awed and a little excited.

"This is ridiculous!" Alicia snapped. "Is this some sort of prank? What on earth are you all talking about?"

Ethyl Marilyn Johnson stood suddenly. "I don't have to tolerate this."

The policeman stood. "Nilah, does your *source* know where the brooch is?"

A chair went skidding across the floor, banging into a wall causing Alicia to squeal and Justine to flinch in reaction. "Tell him!" Lizzie's ghost seemed to be jumping up and down.

Meanwhile, Beth stood in place and watched everything that was happening with a huge grin on her face. "Wow. Level one phenomena... Go Granny, go!" she cheered.

The words seemed to spurn Lizzie on. The lights continued their frantic flashing, the stack of papers went airborne, and Franklin's coffee mug flew off the table and shattered against the wall.

"Level three!" Beth shouted over the pandemonium.

"Lizzie cut it out!" I snapped, uncaring what anyone thought. "Someone's going to get hurt! The lights stopped their flashing and the papers fluttered to the floor. "Sheesh," I sighed. "To answer your question, Officer Casper, I was told that the missing brooch is pinned on a chain under Mrs. Johnson's sweater, and my source insists that it's still there. Right now."

Ethyl Johnson, who'd been cowering behind her family when items started flying, suddenly froze in place. "Don't any of you touch me!" She hissed, backing up against the wall.

"Aunt Marilyn?" Justine gasped. "That can't be true!"

Before anyone else could react, Beth reached over and grabbed at the neckline of her great-aunt's bulky sweater. With one quick jerk there was a slight popping sound. Beth pulled her hand away, yanking free a large pendant from under the old woman's cardigan.

"*How dare you!*" Ethyl tried to grab the jewelry back from her great-niece.

The heavy silver brooch was indeed pinned to a chain. Under the now steady illumination of the overhead lights of the conference room, the pearls seemed to glow, and the large central blue topaz shimmered.

"You greedy old bitch," Beth said, her voice echoing in the now silent conference room.

"That's my girl!" Lizzie shouted. I did my best not to react to her cheer, but my lips curved into a smile, anyway.

"That jewelry belongs to me!" Ethyl shouted, pressing a hand to her neck. "I'm going to press charges for assault!"

"You do that, and I'll file charges for theft!" Justine said firing up. "I imagine the Fogg's could add some complaints to that as well. Like say, insurance fraud?"

I stepped farther away from the family and ranged myself by the door. The three women began to shout back and forth, but before things could get any more heated; Officer Casper neatly stepped between the women. "Would you like to press charges at this time?" he said to Justine and Beth, pointedly ignoring the older woman.

Justine seemed to think about it for a moment, then she shook her head. "No," she said. "We'll keep this *misunderstanding*, in the family." Justine turned to Franklin. "I am so sorry about this Franklin. If you are satisfied, we will let the entire matter drop."

"Of course." Franklin nodded.

"We'll just see about this!" Ethyl Marilyn

Johnson began to storm out of the conference room. "I'm going to contact my lawyer!"

"Floozy," I coughed as she flounced past me.

She whipped her head around and glared at me. "*What* did you say to me?"

"You heard me." I said as the woman's mouth opened and closed several times. "Your sister Lizzie says hello," I added quietly, watching as her eyes grew large. "Oh, and by the way she thinks your sweater is hideous."

CHAPTER EIGHT

Funny how quickly people want you to leave—when you've done something that freaks them out. After Ethyl Johnson stormed out of the conference room, Lizzie vanished. Alicia stared at me as if I'd grown two heads then told me to go back to my office, immediately. Franklin went into 'cover your ass' mode attempting to schmooze and smooth things over with Justine and Beth.

However, before I could withdraw, Lizzie's daughter, Justine, pulled me close and cried on my shoulder. Justine was understandably emotional, but relieved to have her mothers brooch returned. "Thank you," she said. "I don't know how you made all of this happen. But thank you."

I patted her back. "You're very welcome."

Turned out that Lizzie's family were huggers. As soon as her mother released me, Beth pounced. "Nilah, me and you, we need to talk. Soon," she said under her breath.

I returned the hug. "Sure. If I don't get fired for this." I whispered.

Beth let me go and her blue eyes were lit up. "Oh trust me, you don't have to worry about that."

"I'm happy to have helped," I said loud enough for everyone to hear.

"Thank you. Again," Justine said clutching her mother's brooch. "Nilah, thank you so much."

I nodded and with my heart pounding, went straight back up to my office. I expected that Lizzie would be waiting for me when I got there, and was disappointed that she was nowhere to be seen. I attempted to go about my regular work, figuring that any moment Alicia would come barging in my office and tell me to clear out my desk.

But she didn't. No one in the building called me either, which was odd. Usually I fought to get work done in between inter-office phone calls. But I was left alone for the rest of the afternoon.

The silence did nothing to relieve my anxiety or the tension that had my muscles coiled and ready to react. When five o'clock rolled around it was sort of anti-climatic. I shut down my computer, gathered up my purse and jacket and left the building. I didn't think it was a coincidence that I didn't see anyone on my way out. I let myself out the employee entrance, walked stiffly down the little sidewalk on the way to the parking lot and stopped dead at the sight of Old Joe's ghost pruning the flowers.

He tipped his cap. "You did well today."

Keep moving, Nilah! I thought, forcing myself to continue forward. "So, you know about that?"

"Sure, Lizzie was here a bit ago. She told me."

Figures. I thought sourly. *Ghosts will talk to each other, but not to the person whose job or reputation they put at risk.* "Walk with me," I said, as I continued forward. I didn't see him 'move' but suddenly he appeared next to my car, waiting for me.

"Did you speak to my grandson?"

I rooted in my purse for my keys. "I tried." I surveyed the immediate area, making sure we were alone before saying anything else. "It didn't go over too well. He didn't believe me."

"He'll come around. I've seen to that. Don't you worry."

"Believe me, that's the last thing I'm worried about right now."

"Remember what I told you. The white rose in the shed. Show him."

"I remember. You don't have to nag." I found

my keys, glanced up, and discovered that I was alone. Again.

I blew out a breath. "Freaking ghosts."

The drive home was brief and I parked behind the shop, turned off the car and simply sat there alone. I leaned my head against the headrest, and let myself take everything in. I tried to take a few deep breaths, and continued reciting the major arcana. *The Hermit, The Wheel of Fortune, Justice...*

The sound of someone clearing their throat had me jumping hard in reaction.

Did we kick ass in there or what?" Lizzie said, sitting next to me in the passenger seat of the car.

"Damn it Lizzie!" I pressed my hands to my heart. "I waited for you at work, wondered why you didn't show up."

"I had things to take care of," Lizzie announced.

I took a deep breath, and willed my heart rate to slow down. "Between you and Old Joe, I think my chances of a heart attack before Halloween are very real."

"Aw, don't be mad." She grinned at me. "We taught that two bit floozy a hard lesson."

Despite myself I had to laugh. "I suppose we did."

"Listen, before I go..." Lizzie sounded very serious all of the sudden. "I simply wanted to say, thank you for helping my family."

"Go?" I asked turning to face her. "What do you mean, *go?*"

"You know what I mean." Lizzie folded her hands in her lap. "Gotta catch my train onto the next destination, so to speak," she said, looking even less *there.*

"Wait," I said, reaching out as she faded before my eyes. "Lizzie don't go."

"I'm proud of you, girl." Lizzie blew me a kiss and was gone.

"Damn it," I said to the now empty seat. "I'll miss you, Lizzie." Tears welled up in my eyes, and I gripped the steering wheel, as a couple of tears spilled over. I began to tremble in reaction to everything that had happened. *I guess holding myself so tight for a extended period of time had a price,* I thought, trying to breathe my way through it. After a few moments, the shaking subsided.

I was trying to re-learn how to breathe regularly when a knock on my driver's side window had me shrieking in surprise.

Joseph Serafin was bent at the waist and peering in through my window. "Hey, are you okay?" He opened my door and reached out. "Why are you crying?"

I grabbed my bag, climbed out of my car without his help, and stood to face him. My eyes traveled up, up, and farther still to meet his. "It's been a hell of a day." I wiped my tears away and frowned at him. "Why are you here?"

"I dropped by the shop to let Sabina know that her replacement part is here and arranged a time tomorrow to repair her stove."

I shut the car door with a bit more force than was necessary. "Great." I faked a smile, ignored my wobbly knees, and tried to nudge him out of the way. "Excuse me," I said pointedly.

He didn't budge.

"What?" I asked crossly.

"While I was in the shop, two women came in to speak to your grandmother."

I rolled my eyes. "You know it's funny, but that sort of thing happens on a fairly regular basis at the psychic parlor."

Joseph invaded my personal space by stepping too close and leaning over me. I automatically backed up against the car. "The two women," he said. "Had recently come from the Fogg Funeral Home." He pressed a little closer, searching my eyes with his.

I sniffled and cast my eyes down. "Okay." *Must have been Justine and Beth,* I figured, which made me sad about Lizzie leaving, all over again.

"Seemed they had a lot to say about you, a stolen brooch, and the ghost of their relative."

"Like I said, it's been a hell of a day." I pushed away from the car and now he stepped back, allowing me to pass.

"Your grandmother and I talked." His words had me pausing.

I considered him from over my shoulder, waiting to hear what he'd say next.

He walked up, stopping a few feet away. "She told me that your gifts *are* new and that you didn't have a lot of experience with them yet."

Exasperated, I turned to face him fully. "I told you that myself the other night!"

"You did."

"So what made you change your mind?"

"I've been living in my grandfather's house for a few months now. When I went home yesterday I found that items had been rearranged, and moved in a very deliberate way."

"What, like vandalism? Did someone break in?"

Joseph frowned. "No. Nothing was broken or taken... this was more like a message."

I sighed. "Well he did tell me he'd *see to it* that you'd come around. I guess he's been trying to get his point across."

"Huh, maybe..." Joseph blinked in surprise at my words.

I tossed up my hands. "So why come to me if you don't want to listen? What do you want?"

"Let's just say that I'm starting to believe you now."

"Well, yippee."

His lips curved at my dry tone. "What has my grandfather been saying to you, exactly?"

"Well at first he kept saying how you and I should meet. Playing matchmaker I suppose." I shrugged. "Then lately he talked about you and about finding a white rose in the shed."

Joseph shook his head over that. "There aren't any roses growing around the garden shed."

I shrugged. "Maybe that's symbolic?"

"Come with me," Joseph said.

"Wait, what?"

"Come with me, to my house. I want you to help me with this."

I checked the sky, the sun would be setting soon, "We don't have a lot of daylight left."

"It's right here in town," Joseph said. "Won't take long."

Which is how I found myself, still wearing my work uniform, standing in the pretty backyard of Joseph Serafin's home at sunset. The house he'd inherited from his grandfather was charming. It was a small cottage-style one and a half story home with white siding and freshly painted dark blue trim.

"This is a nice space." I smiled at the brick paver patio and outdoor furniture. The backyard was surrounded by a privacy fence with a good sized vegetable garden in the back left corner of the yard. A metal shed was next to the garden.

"I've been trying to maintain the yard and garden. Had so many tomatoes this year. I gave a lot of them to the neighbors." Joseph shook his head. "I don't know what I'll do with the pumpkins."

I could see a few small orange pumpkins still on the vine, even though most of the plants were frost burnt and faded. But there were no rosebushes in the entire yard. Together we walked down a brick path lined with solar lights, towards the shed and garden.

Joseph stopped at the gate of the vegetable plot. "He was so proud of this garden."

I glanced up at him. Saw that he was struggling to hold in his emotions. "Old Joe told me that he died here."

"He did," Joseph sighed. "I came over after work. We were going to grill some burgers and have a few beers... and I found him." Joseph's face was set, as he planted his hands on his hips and surveyed the garden. "I wish I would have been here earlier. Maybe he wouldn't have died. He sure as hell wouldn't have been alone."

Acting on impulse I looped my arm through Joseph's. "Your *dziadzio*, said to me after doing two tours of Vietnam that it didn't upset him to have 'kicked off' in his vegetable garden."

Joseph tilted his head silently questioning the Polish word.

"*Dziadzo*—grandpa." I translated.

Joseph chuckled at that. "He always tossed Polish words and phrases at me when I was a kid. My mother always said to humor him and play along like I understood."

"Well that explains a few things." I gave Joseph's arm a squeeze, hoping to make him smile. "For the past two months he's had me scrambling to translate every time I saw him."

"When you said that to me the other night, it scared me a little. But it also made me happy," Joseph said. "You know, because I was hoping that he was still around, in some way."

"Oh he is, don't you worry about that," I said, and then told Joseph how his grandfather had popped in on me in the file room making me bounce off of the file cabinets.

The corners of his eyes crinkled as he listened and, for a second, I thought he might kiss me. Then his gaze was caught and he focused over my head at something else.

"What?" I asked, instinctively turning to see what had caught his attention. A pair of male and female cardinals perched on the roof of the shed. They chirped back and forth at each other.

"They are probably wondering when you are going to fill up the feeders." I'd noticed a few fancy birdfeeders around the back patio. They'd all been empty.

"You said a white rose by the shed?" Joseph asked me.

"Ah actually," I thought about it. "Your grandfather said *the white rose in the shed.*" I jolted hard remembering something important. "No wait. That's not right. There was more." Excited, I grabbed for his hand. "Joseph his exact words were that he'd *left you a little something extra in the garden shed.*"

Joseph marched over to the shed doors and slid them open. The shed was dark and he ducked inside, reaching for his cell phone and using it as a flashlight.

I pulled my phone from my purse and followed him. The shed, though clean was crammed full of gardening equipment and tools. Running around the top of the shed on three sides was a metal shelf with stacks of vintage motor oil cans arranged side by side. "Wow, so Old Joe collected antique motor oil cans."

"He did." Joseph nodded. "But as you can see there are no roses or any plants growing in the shed."

"Let me get back in there," I said. Joseph ducked back outside and I stepped in, shining my light onto the vintage cans. "You know, some of these motor oil cans might be valuable."

As soon the words left my mouth, my stomach flipped over. I listened with half an ear while Joseph commented that he was going to do some research on the cans this winter, and instead of paying attention to him, I focused on the artwork on the cans.

In the far right hand corner of the shelf, a bright yellow motor oil can with red letters seemed to stand out like a beacon. The can read *White Rose Motor Oil.*

"Joseph," I interrupted him.

"What's wrong?"

"Shine your phone's light over in the far right corner."

"What do you see?" Joseph's voice was hushed, expectant.

"The yellow can with red lettering," I said. "Look at the name. Check out the *flower* illustrated on the can"

"The White Rose," Joseph breathed. "Well, holy shit," he said, starting to laugh.

Uncaring of the blazer and skirt, I squeezed myself between a garden tiller and several large bags of potting soil. I reached up and pulled the can down from the shelf.

I immediately handed the old can out to Joseph. "Maybe the can is a valuable collectable. I wonder if that's why he wanted you to have it?" I said, climbing back out.

He turned the can over and I shined my phone's light on it. "The bottom of the can has been opened," Joseph said. "Which would make it less valuable."

"Is there anything inside of it?" I wondered out loud.

Joseph handed me his phone, I aimed the light at his hands as he pushed at the bottom of the can. "There *is* something inside." Joseph bent back the metal and pulled out a sealed plastic sandwich bag.

My breath left me in a rush as I saw that inside the clear little bag was a large roll of cash. "Wow," I managed.

Joseph seemed to be struggling with his emotions, as we stood there.

"Maybe we should take this 'little something extra' inside?" I suggested gently.

CHAPTER NINE

I sat at the kitchen table in Joseph's house and one hundred dollar bills were spread out across the little table. There were seventy-five of them.

"That's seven thousand, five hundred dollars," I said, with a giggle. "In. Cash." I'd probably repeated myself several times but I didn't care.

Joseph was pacing back and forth, talking on the phone with his mother about what we'd found. "I don't care what the will states," he said to her. "You and dad should take the money and—"

I smiled, as his mother argued with him over the phone. A short time later the call was finished and he ran an aggravated hand through his hair. "She won't listen. I told her the money should be for her, but she keeps insisting that the will clearly states—"

"That the house, shed, surrounding property and all of its *contents* is bequeathed to you." I finished for him. "I could hear your mom."

He made a grumbling sound of frustration. "What the hell am I supposed to do with the money?"

"I agree with your mom," I said, grinning at him. "Put it back into the house." I considered the old cabinets and worn kitchen countertops. "It's a great house but it does need some freshening up."

Joseph sat across from me. "I was sort of thinking about replacing the kitchen counters, or gutting the upstairs bathroom. It's got baby blue tile on the walls, and the sink is too low for me..." he trailed off. "But I didn't have the cash for the remodel."

"Well you do now." I patted his hand. "My brother Vincent is a general contractor, he could probably help you out with the bathroom."

Joseph started to gather up the cash. "Maybe I should talk to your brother. I would want to do a lot of the work myself, though." He rolled up the bills and put them back in the bag, and inside of the motor oil can once again. He paused for a moment and finally stuck the can in the pantry.

I stood up, unsure of what to do now. I mean

was there a protocol for this type of thing? *Hey I know we only met a few days ago... but I'm glad the message from your deceased grandfather worked out.* I frowned as I considered my options. *What the hell was I supposed to say to him? Live long and prosper? Let's have dinner sometime? So long sexy man-beast?* I finally settled for, "I should probably head home."

Joseph crossed his arms over his chest, leaned back against the fridge, and raised an eyebrow at me. He said nothing, but his expression had my insides tangling in a knot.

I stayed where I was, my insides quaking, and waited. But he didn't speak. Figuring that he was probably a little overwhelmed, I scooped up my purse where it rested on the counter by the back door. "Well," I said. "See you around Joseph." I gave him a friendly wave and let myself out the back door.

I went quickly around the back of the house, and out to the front where my car was parked in the driveway, berating myself the entire way. *What did you think would happen Nilah? That he would be so overcome with gratitude and lust that he'd fulfill your fantasies right there on the spot?*

"A girl can dream," I grumbled to myself. I sighed in disappointment and rooted for my keys, only to drop them. I bent over to pick them up and when I stood, Joseph was right beside me. I squeaked in surprise, pressing a hand to my heart. "Damn! You're a quiet one."

"Nilah," he said. "You left before I could figure out how to say thank you."

"Oh." *Don't act like an idiot around the man!* I told myself. "You're welcome," I said politely, and took a steadying breath.

Once again, Joseph was standing a tad too close, and invading my personal space. I backed up slightly and came up short against the side of my car. He didn't say anything, instead he leaned down and seemed to be searching my face.

"Joseph, do you need glasses or something?" I put a hand on his chest to put some distance between us. "Quit looming over me."

"Can't help but loom over folks. I'm always taller than everyone else." He smiled, and stepped even closer.

I started to chuckle at that, but then his thighs brushed against my skirt. I gulped nervously. Standing in the dark with him I watched as the wind tugged at his long hair. *What was it about men with longer hair?* I wondered. *Between that and the trimmed beard, it was... well, for lack of a better word. Tribal.* Caught in his gaze, I stood there, my hand on his chest, simply staring up at him. My heart began to beat faster. *Was he finally going to kiss me?*

He tipped my chin up. "You look tired," he said.

"Wow, thanks." Fantasy ruined, I tried to yank my head back.

"Stand still a minute." He stopped me by gently sliding his fingers from under my chin, to around the back of my head. "I *meant* that this has been hard on you. It's made you tired."

"It has. So let me go, and I'll head on home." I tried to sound firm but my voice was husky.

"Nope." He tugged me a little closer.

"Listen, man-beast I'm not sure what sort of woman you are used to dealing with—"

He threw back his head and laughed. "Man beast?"

Oh shit! Did I say that out loud? I reached up, attempting to bat his hand away.

"It's safe to say I've never dealt with a woman like you before," he said, tightening his grip. Then he moved in.

I only had a second to react. Sure I could have said no. But with all six feet four inches of sexiness swooping down, I managed to suck in a quick breath right before his mouth landed on mine.

And then I gave as good as I got.

I reached up and grabbed a handful of his hair. For once in my life I was in a man's arms who made me feel smaller, feminine and also a tiny bit afraid. The thrill of the unknown, and that hint of fear only added to the rush. This was no tentative kiss. It was a delicious exploration, and maybe a challenge all rolled into one.

He threaded his hands through the back of my hair, pulling the updo loose. Bobby pins scattered and hit the ground. I nipped his bottom lip, urging him on. He bent my head back from the force of his kiss, and I found myself being picked up straight off the driveway.

My feet were dangling, and then he pressed me against the car. It seemed like he could hold me like that forever. The fact that he was strong enough to do so turned me on even more.

If such a thing was possible.

For a few moments I forgot everything. That I was making out in public, that the neighbors could step out and see us any moment, or even what my own name was. This was insane. This was thrilling. This had to stop, or better yet, continue somewhere else in private.

We broke apart from each other gasping for breath. He set me back on my feet, by letting me slide down the front of his body. It left no doubt in my mind that he was as aroused by the kiss as I was. We both stood with our eyes locked on each other, panting in the driveway.

"Well," I said. "I should probably go."

"Probably," he agreed and ran a hand gently down the side of my face.

I reached blindly for the car door. Opened it

and climbed inside. I started to close the door. "See you around, Joseph." I managed to say in a almost normal tone of voice.

"See you soon." He nodded and shut the door.

How in the hell I managed to drive myself back to my apartment and not get lost, was a freaking miracle.

***

The next few days passed quickly for me. Word spread throughout Danvers of the 'ghostly incident' at the funeral parlor. I received an email from Franklin Fogg informing me that due to recent events, I was on unpaid administrative leave until further notice. So while they didn't come straight out and fire me, I was for all intents and purposes, laid off. I put in applications for adjunct teaching positions at the local community college and hoped I'd hear something for the January semester.

Typically at this time of year, the town gossip was centered on who was taking who to the Halloween Gala. However, the story of Lizzie's ghost combined with whispers of my involvement in the recovery of the stolen jewelry and my subsequent 'administrative leave' were running a close second.

Babcia simply told me to ignore the gossip, as not all of it was pleasant, and to keep my head up. Some people claimed I was like a supernatural crime solver, and others whispered that I was merely a troublemaker, hoping for attention. A few people had actually asked me if I was available for Medium style readings. I said that I would think about it.

With Halloween only a few days away, Madame Sabina's was crazy busy. I figured if nothing else, helping out at the shop during the busiest week of the year was a good way to earn some cash. If my being there brought in more curious people...well, then that would help boost sales.

Vanessa was seriously miffed at my being the center of attention. She decreed that I was fit to run the cash register, so while she flitted about the shop and scheduled Madame Sabina's readings, I manned the front counter.

After the months of the funeral home's suffocating quiet, the action of the shop was like a rejuvenating shot in the arm. It was loud, jam-packed with locals and Halloween season tourists. And I found myself enjoying it, much more than I'd expected.

Now I could wear whatever the hell I wanted, and I was taking full advantage of that. Today, I had chosen a swing style dress in vertical lines of burgundy and white tie dye. Its scooped neck and long sleeves were flattering, as was the jagged edged hem that ended right above my knees. I had paired it with some over-the-knee suede black boots, and left my hair long and loose. A pair of orange enameled jack o' lantern earrings swung from my ears, and a matching necklace hung around my neck.

I was ringing up a set of reproduction Gypsy-Witch tarot cards for a customer when I glanced up and found Beth, Lizzie's granddaughter, standing in line at the counter. She was chic and comfortable in dark jeans, and a hilarious black sweatshirt that featured a cute ghost with the words, *Boo, Bitches!* on it.

"Hey Beth!" I smiled over at her.

"Wow, girl, I almost didn't recognize you!"

I had to laugh. "Thanks."

"Can I talk to you?" Beth asked, brushing at her sunny, inverted bob haircut.

"Sure, let me finish up here."

A few minutes later and the customer was happily leaving with her purchase. I moved out from behind the counter and made my way over to where Beth was admiring some Baltic amber jewelry in a case.

"How's your family?" I asked her.

"They're doing okay," Beth said.

"I suppose you have some questions for me after the other day," I said, and even though I had expected this—I still found it a little embarrassing.

"I do. But first I want to know something." Beth spotted Vanessa hovering and trying to cavesdrop. "Hi Vanessa!" she said brightly to my sister. "I'm gonna steal Nilah here for a moment. She'll be right back." Beth latched onto my arm and tugged me out and on the sidewalk.

"I'll be back," I called to Vanessa, biting my lip to keep from laughing.

Beth linked her arm through mine and we started to stroll off down the tourist filled sidewalk. "So," she began. "I heard through the grapevine that you are on administrative leave from Fogg Funeral Home."

I nodded. "That's correct."

"They shouldn't be able to do that to you," Beth said firmly. "I want you to know that both my mother and I came to see Sabina after the incident and she filled us in on your Medium abilities, and how you are still learning."

I nodded, and let her continue to talk.

"We also both tried to call Franklin Fogg and register a complaint at their treatment of you," Beth announced.

"You did?" I blinked at that.

"We tried, and so did several other members of our family, but we never got through to Franklin directly."

It's okay," I said to her. "Tell your family that I appreciate the effort." We walked along for a little while in silence. "You know Beth, I said. "You really remind me of Lizzie."

"God, I miss her." Beth's voice caught on her words.

"I wasn't trying to make you sad. She adored you. She told me you watched ghost hunting shows with her, and that she *knew the lingo*."

At my words, Beth threw back her head and laughed. "God, she was the most—"

"Bad-ass Granny," we said simultaneously.

"Could you see her, in the conference room the other day?" Beth wanted to know.

"Yes," I admitted. "She told me she wanted to give everyone a show. She was bouncing up and down waving her arms at me and, as you saw, sending things flying around the room."

"That's my girl." Beth wiped a tear from her eye.

I grinned at her. "Funny you should say that. She shouted the exact same thing about you, when you yanked that brooch out from under Ethyl's sweater."

Beth stopped and gave me an enthusiastic hug. "Thank you for that."

I squeezed her back. "It was my pleasure," I said, and meant it.

"So anyway," Beth said as we walked further along. "Seeing as you need a job, I was wondering if you'd like to come work for me."

I stopped on the sidewalk. "Work for you?"

"Yes, It'd be part time to start," Beth explained. I need an assistant for my business, typing, filing, answering the phone and interviewing prospective clients..."

I listened as she rattled off an hourly wage. "So, noon to 8:00 pm on Tuesday's, Thursday's, and Saturday's?" I repeated back, a little shocked.

"That's right," she said. "I believe you are uniquely qualified, and I need someone with both knowledge *and* experience in the field."

"What field?" I asked.

"Paranormal investigations." Beth answered completely seriously. "I run DPI. Danvers Paranormal Investigations."

***

Vanessa had worked herself into a fine state by the time Beth and I arrived back at the shop an hour later. My grandmother was standing on the sales floor talking to a few customers and her face lit up when we walked in.

"So, it is all settled then?" she said directly to me. "You took the job?"

Beth shook her head and grinned at Madame Sabina. "I'm not going to insult you by asking how you knew. Instead I'm going to request that you'll consider consulting with us on investigations in the future."

"Yes!" My grandmother clapped her hands

together in excitement. "Yes, I would...so long as it's not during my busy time of the year."

"That's a deal!" Beth winked at her and stuck out her hand to me. "I'll see you the day after Halloween."

I smiled and shook her hand. "I'm looking forward to it!"

After the shop closed up for the night I made my way up to my apartment. The orange and purple lights above my window and the foam pumpkins on the sill cast a creepy and festive light over my apartment. Squash meowed loudly, complaining of my absence and to make up for it, I spent the next fifteen minutes tossing his toys for him around the apartment. The cat made a spectacular leap off the back of the sofa for his green felt fish when someone knocked on my door.

I opened it to find a smiling Joseph Serafin on my landing holding a brown paper grocery bag. "Hello," I said, very surprised.

"Nilah, you look great."

"You're not so bad, yourself," I said, admiring his gray button down shirt and a pair of dark slacks. I'd never seen him so nicely dressed. "Won't you come in?"

Joseph stepped in and surveyed my apartment's colorful décor. "I really like your place," he said.

"Thank you," I said. "What's in the bag?"

"Here," he handed me the bag and it was surprisingly heavy. "I thought you might like to have one."

I peered down and discovered a pumpkin with a long trailing stem. "From your grandfather's garden?"

"Yeah, I figured I'd carve up the other pumpkins for my house for the trick-or-treaters, and give one to you. I think my grandfather would approve."

"This is great. Thanks," I said, and set the bag aside on my kitchen table. I gestured towards the sofa. "Would you like to sit down?"

He sat, and I joined him on the sofa. I crossed my legs and couldn't help but notice that Joseph was staring at them. Testing, I smoothed the dress down over my thighs and was rewarded with seeing a little twitch in reaction. *Well, well,* I thought. *Isn't that interesting?*

Before I could do anything else, Squash introduced himself by jumping onto Joseph and spitting his green felt fish in his lap. "Cool tabby cat." Joseph ran a hand over the cat's ears, sending him into kitty ecstasy. "What's his name?" he asked over the loud purrs.

"Squash."

Joseph started to laugh. "Seriously? You named your cat, Squash?"

"I thought it was more dignified than Pumpkin," I said reasonably.

"So..." Joseph tossed the fish and Squash leapt into action. "I heard you lost your job at the funeral home."

I smirked. "They are calling it 'unpaid administrative leave'."

"That's bullshit," Joseph said. "What are you going to do now?"

"It just so happens I was offered a new job today."

"Really?"

"Yup," I said as Squash jumped to the coffee table. In his excitement, the cat knocked that old deck of tarot cards off the table, and they hit the floor, spilling out of their box. "Nice move, Squash." I shook my head.

"A new job doing what?" Joseph asked and bent to help pick up the cards.

I knelt down besides the table and began pushing the cards back in the box. "Assisting the owner of Danvers Paranormal Investigations."

He handed me a few more of the fallen cards. "Well that's perfect for you."

"I think it could be," I agreed, setting the box aside and reaching way under the table for the last card.

Joseph stood and offered me a hand up. "Maybe you could tell me more about that, over dinner."

I took his hand and rose to my feet. "Are you asking me out on a date?"

"I am," Joseph said. "I thought it would be good for us to get to know each other better."

I turned the last tarot card over to see what it was. The results had my heart bumping hard in surprise. "Yes, I'd love going to dinner," I said, laughing. "In fact, I think that's probably a wise idea all things considered."

Joseph inclined his head towards the card. "Okay, that laugh tells me—you *know* something. But I didn't think that you read tarot cards."

"Technically, I don't. But I'm a Gypsy at heart, and almost everyone knows the definition of *this* card."

"Show me," Joseph said quietly.

I raised my eyebrows. "You sure you want to know?"

"Yes," he said.

I flipped the card over, and held it face up for him to see.

The tarot card portrayed a man and woman sharing an intimate moment in a beautiful garden. Above and behind the twosome, and emerging from the clouds, a winged angel watched over the pair. The light of the sun seemed to illuminate the scene, and the angel that was reaching out as if to bless the couple, who were on the verge of a kiss.

The card I held was *The Lovers*.

The End.

Turn the page for a sneak peek at the next sexy installment of The Gypsy Chronicles.
Gypsy Spirit
Coming Fall 2017

EXCERPT
GYPSY SPIRIT

I leaned against my doorframe dressed only in a black satin nightie and smiled as my lover grabbed a last cup of coffee before heading out for his day. *You have to admit,* I thought as I watched, *it was a hell of a view.*

Joseph Serafin, all buff and brawny six foot four inches of him, rested a hip against my kitchen counter, sampled his coffee and grinned back at me as I yawned. His denim blue shirt was still unbuttoned allowing glimpses of a splendidly broad chest. His brown hair fell casually to the tops of his shoulders, while his beard was neatly trimmed. He looked exactly like what he was, a sexy man-beast... and he was all mine.

"Tired?" he asked, raising one eyebrow.

"You didn't let me get much sleep last night," I told him, and ran a hand through my long brown hair. It was probably sticking straight up in the air after having his hands in it most of the night… either from him smoothing it back from my face as he lavished kisses on me, or from yanking my head back by my hair as he held me firmly in place, while he plundered.

God the man was good at plundering. I shuddered.

I saw movement out of the corner of my eye. Squash, my orange tabby cat, sat on the back of the couch staring out the window in the break in the curtains. I felt a little tingle of sensation and checked again. *Was that a shimmer of light in the corner of the living room? What was causing that?*

My thoughts were distracted as Joseph turned to me, and I got a full view of him standing there in his jeans and unbuttoned shirt. My mouth watered. Even after a year together the man made my hormones go crazy. I calculated how much time he had before he had his first appointment for the day.

I stood up a little straighter, and one strap slid off my shoulder. "Oops." I said as if I was surprised.

Joseph's gaze zeroed in. "Don't distract me, woman."

"Sorry." I shrugged, and glanced down.

The nightie was starting to slowly slide off the

slope of my breast. The fabric clung, defying gravity, and the fact that I had big boobs to begin with only made the inevitable slide a little slower. I leaned back a bit against the doorframe stretched, and wondered what he would do.

He sent me a slow burning look out of those fabulous brown eyes. My belly clenched. *I knew that look.* "Nilah." His voice was husky and low.

"Yes?" The nightie began to slide further. I smiled, slowly.

The coffee cup hit the counter with a snap. In two steps he was in front of me. His mouth landed on mine, and I reached up and grabbed a handful of his long hair. He snagged me around the waist and lifted me. I wrapped my legs around his waist and the next thing I knew he had slung me to the kitchen counter.

My shoulders hit the painted cabinets, and I groaned my delight in his mouth. While I tried to shove his shirt off his shoulders, I heard him unbuckling and unzipping. His mouth slid from my mouth, to my throat, and he latched on to my breast.

"Joseph!" I demanded, reaching back and wrapping my hands around his amazing ass, I tugged him closer to me.

Standing between my thighs, he angled his hips and slammed into me. Just the way I liked it. He leaned down over me and held still for a moment. Eye to eye, our hearts beat in unison, and I felt him stretch me tight as he pressed even deeper inside of me.

I let out a little scream and that spurned him on. With a deep growl, he bent my knees further apart, and began to thrust. I heard a crash, as a few dishes were knocked from the counter to the floor, and the thump of my back hitting the cabinets as we took each other.

It wasn't long before I was shouting from my orgasm, and his release soon followed. We sprawled there and fought to catch our breath. Our eyes met and we grinned at each other, and then we began to laugh.

"Damn it Nilah, I'm going to be late," he grumbled.

"I didn't do anything," I said. "I was just standing there."

"Ha!" he laughed, and rubbed his beard across the sensitive skin of my breasts.

I shrieked and yanked his ear in retaliation. In revenge, he bit down on the upper slope of my breast and began to suck.

"Don't you dare give me a hickey!" I said, trying not to laugh.

He lifted his head and I felt the slight sting. "Just marking my territory." He dropped a playful kiss on the mouth and released me.

"Barbarian," I teased him.

Joseph walked over to the bath to clean up. I stayed where I was on the counter with my legs dangling off the side and tried to talk myself into moving.

I managed to tug my nightie back down over the tops of my thighs. Joseph strolled out of the bathroom all buttoned up. He tugged his boots on, gathered up his things in record time, grabbed his jacket and stopped to give me a kiss. I wrapped my fingers in his hair and held on. He lingered over the kiss long enough that I thought maybe he might stay.

I made a sound of disappointment when he stepped away.

He headed for the door, stopped and glanced over his shoulder at me. "I want you waiting for me just like that, when I get here tonight."

I raised my eyebrows. "Really? Is that an order or a request?"

"Order." He grinned.

"And if I don't?" I asked tartly.

The smile he sent me was devastating. "There will be *consequences*." He drew the last word out.

My stomach quivered. "Oh yeah?" I tossed my head at the challenge. "Is that a threat or a promise?"

"Both," he winked at me and let himself out the door.

I swung my legs for a moment and then eased

down from the counter. I headed to the bathroom to shower and clean up. Afterwards, I wrapped myself in a plush robe and fished out the disinfectant wipes from under the kitchen sink to wipe down the counter top.

Humming to myself, I picked up the dishes that had been knocked over during our romp, and threw the wipes in the garbage. I straightened up and turned towards the living room. What I saw there had me screaming in horror.

Alicia Fogg my former boss, and the richest and biggest bitch in town, stood in my living room scowling at me...and she didn't look so good. Her silk blouse was rumpled and stained, her hair was a mess, and she was deathly pale.

I pressed my hands to my galloping heart. "What in the holy hell are *you* doing here?"

I need your help," Alicia said, her voice raspy.

"How did you get in?" I demanded.

"I'm not sure..."

"Get out of my house!" I snapped.

"I can't. I don't even know how I got here." Alicia whined.

I marched over to her intending to grab the woman by the arm and throw her bodily out the door—and my hand went right through her shoulder.

A chill ran down my back. "Oh shit." I said recoiling from the spirit.

"What's going on?" she said, looking more shocked than me. "I've been wandering around for days, trying to find someone to help me... and then I found myself drawn here." Alicia's bottom lip trembled. "Am I a ghost?"

I tossed my hands in the air. "Looks like."

"I'm dead, then." Alicia looked around forlornly.

"I thought I had the place warded against roaming spirits," I groused. "You shouldn't be able to get in."

"Why am I *here*?" she wanted to know. "I don't understand how I got here."

"Probably because I'm the only one who *can* communicate with you."

"That can't be right. I don't even like you." Alicia snapped.

"Back at ya baby." I snapped. Then a horrible thought occurred to me. "How long have you actually been here?"

"For a while..." she said and then turned up her nose. "You were too busy with that disgusting display to notice.

Now I was truly horrified. "You *watched* us, you perv?"

"Not by choice. She crossed her arms over her chest. "The kitchen counter? Really Nilah. That is so low class."

"Get out!" I pointed towards the door.

"I tried!" Alicia's bottom lip appeared to tremble. "I'm afraid I might be stuck here."

"Not for long if I have anything to say about it," I grumbled.

My name is Nilah Stephanik. I come from a long line of *Polska Roma* fortune tellers, mystics, and psychics. I'd always thought I had no occult talents of any kind...that is until about a year ago.

I learned the hard way to be very careful what you wish for, because it ended up that I'm actually a Psychic Medium, and unfortunately, I can communicate with the dead.

Whether I want to or not.

Gypsy Spirit
Book 2 of The Gypsy Chronicles Series
Coming Fall 2017

ABOUT ELLEN DUGAN

Ellen Dugan is the award winning author of twenty three books. A psychic-clairvoyant, she has been a practicing Witch for over thirty years. Well known for her candor and humor, she is also a Master Gardener. Ellen's popular magickal books have been translated into over twelve foreign languages. In 2015 Ellen launched a popular, paranormal fiction series entitled, Legacy of Magick.

Please visit her website and blog -
www.ellendugan.com and
www.ellendugan.blogspot.com

GLOSSARY OF POLISH TERMS

Babcia (Bahp-chya) — Grandmother

Ddzień dobry (Jean Dough-bree) — Good Morning

Dziadzio (Jah-joh) — Grandpa

Kocham cię (ko-hahm tchiem) — I love you

Kochanie (Ko-han-yeh) — Darling

Miłego dnia (Mee-uego dne-ea) — Have a nice day

Polska Roma (Polska Romah) — Romany Gypsy from Poland

Psychiczna średniej (Psa-he-chna shred-nyee) — Psychic medium

Wnucka (vnoochka) — Granddaughter

Made in the USA
Middletown, DE
31 August 2018